Breaking Away — The Sequel

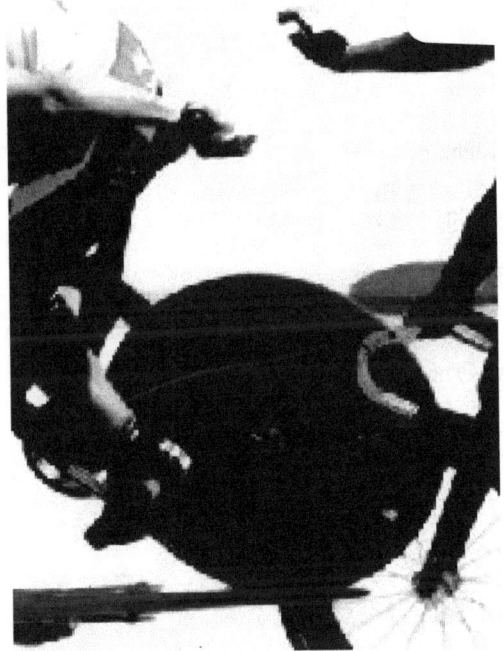

Hand-S-l-i-n-g

Story, Photography and Graphics
by Sandra Wright Sutherland
with a tribute to Jerry Baker

Pre-press production by Sandra Wright Sutherland
using MacBook Air, Pages, Photos, and Preview

First Edition
Printed in the USA

ISBN: 978-0-9645243-2-3

The Iris tri-Logo: the iris flower (nature),
the iris of the camera lens (technology) and
the iris of the human eye (human endeavor).
Iris was the Greek goddess of the rainbow.
The Rainbow Jersey is the highest honor
in the world of bicycle racing.

by Iris Press
105 Westridge Dr
Bozeman, MT 59715
831-601-4831
irispress@aol.com / irispress@gmail.com

Breaking Away -- The Sequel

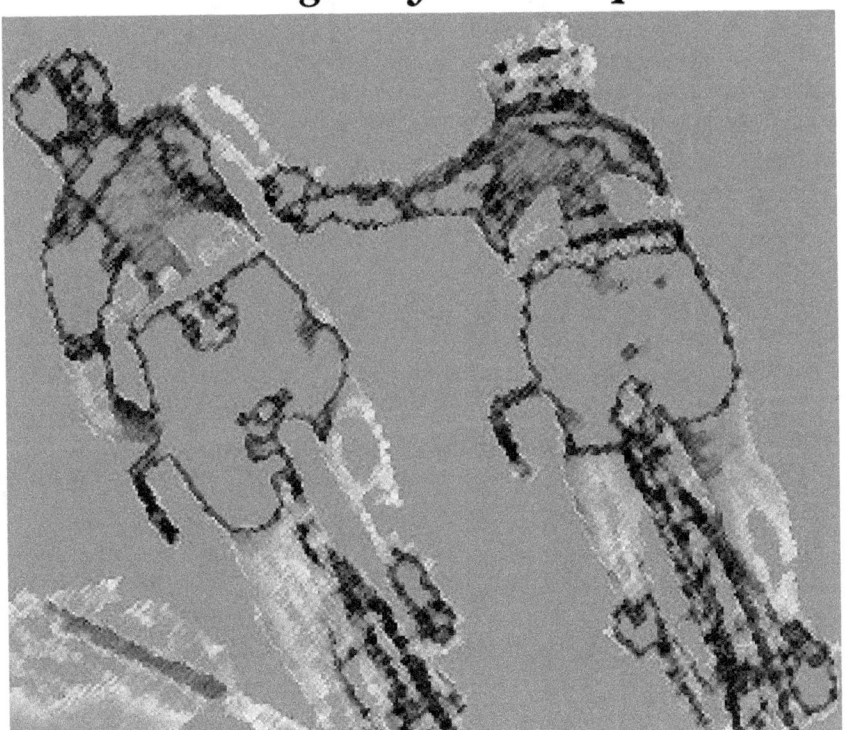

Hand-S-l-i-n-g

In 1979, four boys from Indiana surprised all of Bloomington by winning the Little 500, a race put on by the University. They were allowed to join the race with the expectation that a college fraternity would win. The boys surprised them -- and themselves. Against all odds, including a crash, poor equipment, and inexperience, they won the trophy that the frat boys thought they had locked up.

Since those years long ago, each boy went his separate way. Many of their fans who read about and saw their story wondered where they went and what happened to them. The only person who persisted in maintaining contact was Moocher's wife Nancy, who wrote Christmas cards every year to the other boys and their wives, about Bloomington and the children she and Moocher were raising. If she lost an address, which she often did for Dave and Mike, she pestered the Post Office until the forwarding address was sent. She tracked them down like the many school "reunion" committees. Dave's parents, Mr and Mrs Stohler had maintained contact periodically, too, partly because they were close by, so she knew more about what Dave had done than the others. Ironically, although Cyril wrote constantly as part of his work, it was more often his wife Melody who returned a card at Christmas. Mike was the most difficult to track.

This year, partly by happenstance and partly with intent, the boys each had a son or daughter who was participating in the Marymoor Grand Prix, an annual event held at the Jerry Baker Marymoor Velodrome in Seattle. While Moocher never left Bloomington -- and Nancy only for work demands -- they decided to herd up their brood of five children to make the Trip of a Lifetime with a "special intent" they had been planning for years. The reunion included some ideas that had echoed in Moocher's dreams since that day they won the Little 500, when he had nothing but a crumbling house to offer him shelter. The other boys were like his closest family, his brothers, and he missed them every day. This year, the dream he had carried all these years would be fulfilled. Maybe...

But first, a review of each boy's life, so that readers and *Breaking Away* fans understand how things came to this marvelous point in Seattle on this glorious, sunny day. As each "boy" moves into view, he is accompanied by a review of a life that began in Bloomington all those years ago to this year in Seattle. Knowing what was coming, each "boy" reflected on the past leading to now:

1. Mike

2016. Mike was excited to be at the entry of the Jerry Baker Marymoor velodrome. He watched the bike racers elbow each other for space by the registration table as they dropped their equipment to one side. They looked focused, aggressive, and ready to take on all comers. Ah, Mike remembered what that felt like, the bravado, the surety that you were going to beat the other guy, whatever the sport, that anything was possible -- and he wished he still had that devil-may-care enthusiasm. Some riders had bikes that looked new - and outfits to

4

match, others had bikes that were a little beat up. Most bikes had the lovely simple configuration of track bikes: 1) they had only one gear and 2) NO brakes on the handle bars. Road bikes were only used on a velodrome for warm-up. Mike never did understand having no brakes on these bikes, called "fixies". At least in the Little 500 they had coaster brakes. These bikes had no brakes at all. Riders could only slow the bike by resisting the forward motion of the pedals. Not good for quick stops. Why wouldn't they want brakes on them? Man, the bike switch in the 500 was tough to do, even with a coaster brake. Still, he always loved the simplicity of no derailleur to adjust. He never figured out the shifting, anyway.

One boy had a ratty looking bike, but it was clean as a pin and Mike recognized top flight equipment, even though the boy holding it apparently cared little about the paint job.

That particular boy caught Mike's attention, matching memories of someone he used to know. He had on a green warmup jacket. His hair was longer and not cut in any kind of style. A second boy in line had shorter hair.

"Joey, you got a fiver? I'm short." the boy in the green jacket sounded a little agitated, but friendly.

"You're short, okay..." Joey replied.

"Hey, watch it! Gimme a five, you know I'm good for it. "

Joey handed the other boy a picture of Andrew Jackson.

"Here -- though I know you'd rather have pictures of Benjamin Franklin. You know, if I'm going to keep staking you to entry fees, I'm going to start charging you interest."

"I'll pay you back! I just keep forgetting my checkbook. I thought I had enough cash.

"Oh sure, Chilly, you'll pay me back like you always do. You're just like your old man."

"Leave him out of this, will ya? Okay, take it out of my prize money, you KNOW I'm good for it."

Ah "Chilly". Yes, this would have to be Moocher's boy, the fantastic rider with intuitive gifts when it came to judging other riders and chalking up way more wins way more than most. Mike thought he looked familiar.

"Yeah, that's the ONLY way you're good for it. Lucky you catch enough primes to end up with good bucks. What do you do with it?"

"None of your business." Chilly smiled back, as if he had a great secret.

Joey looked at Chilly's bike.

"Okay, okay... here. I'm glad you found something to keep you motivated so I can get my money back. Doesn't look like you spend money on paint jobs."

"That's my secret weapon!", Chilly replied. "They all have these showroom bikes. They take one look at my bike and think I'm a "Fred". Then I SPRINT by them! And they don't know what hit 'em!" Chilly laughed. "I'm always surprised when it works again and again!"

"Next up??" The lady taking registration forms was looking at them.

The boys handed her their entry forms and money.. What Joey knew was that borrowing money was Chilly's way of saying: "Hey, we're friends. I trust you and when you loan me the money, I know you still trust me." Of course, he'd bring his checkbook if he thought about it -- he just had more important things on his mind — like racing!

Mike recognized this cock-eyed male bonding ritual. It was a kind of love exchange particular to males. The next step was when they punched each other - or fake-punched - just to say "I like you, we're friends."

"Thank you!" crowed the registration lady, trying to keep the line moving. "Two for Madison, one for Keirin. That will be $60 per race. Let me know if you want to add other events."

The boys groaned. It seemed like races were just getting more and more expensive. At the same time, it forced them to "up" their racing strategy so they could win prize money, win primes, or at least place in the top five for a place in the race, maybe getting back their entry fees plus a little more money that they could keep. The trouble was, tires and a wide array of other equipment was also becoming more and more expensive, so they didn't usually end up with much. But the fact was, if they broke even, they were pretty happy about it.

Watching this exchange, Mike saw the familiar face and the familiar routine -- successful because the borrower had endeared himself to the lender. He wondered if that really was Moocher's kid, he thought he recognized the name and was pretty sure. Plus, he looked like Moocher, he had that thin, wiry build Mike knew so well. That would be so cool if his instincts were correct. He loved Moocher and always felt like his big brother, ever since that "fight" they'd had in elementary school. He missed the "Four Musketeers" with a severe nostalgia, ever since life broke away and separated him from his "family" in B-town; from the three boys who were as much brothers as anyone could be, as much or more than his "real" brother.

The memories flooded back. Life frustrated him back then, but he wished he could return to those days, full of uncertainty, but with the security of the companionship of equals who shared his panic at never being good enough. Each of them knew how much they were valued within the group as life hurled on, from high school and into the scary world of a future adulthood. There was no stopping it, though they had tried. When the Cutters won the Little 500, they had no idea what changes were set in motion. It was such a wonderful day, but reliving it also offered a reliving of the last day things made any sense. Soon, Dave and Cyril went off to college and Mike didn't know what he would do. Even though Moocher had next to nothing, Mike owed him a debt he could never repay. He owed Moocher his sanity, maybe his life.

Mike wondered how many other "Cutter kids" would be at this event. He'd heard Moocher's kid was a bike fanatic. So if this was the boy, it wouldn't be a surprise -- sort of. He hoped to see Mooch. He'd lost touch with Dave and Cyril. It seemed like they traveled a lot too. Nancy never wrote nearly enough. She knew how much they all missed each other, even if they didn't hang out any more. The 500 propelled them into new lives, but they'd never really be split up. Either way, it was healthy to move on — except for the jealousy, when everyone seemed to have somewhere to go but Mike. The jealousy never felt good. Mike wondered if anyone of his "brothers" had changed. He knew he had -- a LOT. Or at least he thought so.

"Excuse me, sir, can I squeeze past you here?" A rider waited for him to move aside so he could cross the track with his equipment slung over his shoulder. Mike had been so lost in his reverie that he had lost sight of the rider who reminded him of Moocher. Wonder where he went? Well, that was okay, he was sure he'd see him riding soon. Mike went off to find a good seat. He was going to enjoy this week, watching a sport he'd only seen in snippets or on TV and during that short time in Germany. It looked exciting, all that human-generated speed, spread out right before his eyes. He hadn't seen his daughter in 6 months, and still felt shy about it, so he was happy to just sit in the stands and take in this sport separated by one generation to the single most significant moment of his past. His life had been changed by a track race before, maybe it would be again.

After walking around, Mike settled into a seat on the far side of the track, recalling the path he found all those years ago, more by serendipity than anything else. A path he never imagined, back in the old days.....

Mike's Life Changes...

When Dave got the call to join the CinZano pro cycling team, Mike was happy for him, even though it meant Dave would be leaving Bloomington. Mike knew that racing bikes with the Italians was Dave's dream, and when you love someone, REALLY love them, you want them to fulfill their dream, so he had to be happy, even as he was heartbroken at Dave's loss to his own life. He smiled and congratulated Dave, toasted his good fortune, then went home and cried.

Dave's good fortune didn't help Mike. In fact, nothing could help Mike. For some months, he only felt intense jealousy. He didn't begrudge Dave's good fortune, he begrudged that he couldn't share it. Sure, great, Dave... you're all set. What have I got? NOTHING!

Mike went into a severe depression after Dave got that call from Roberto Simoni, one of the riders who had crashed him. How could Dave forgive that cheater? Mike didn't get it. Dave and Cyril were both going to college, a college Mike couldn't get into. Even Moocher was better off than Mike, he was married, and to a girl who WORKED!

But what was to become of Mike? His "real" brother, Steve, tried to help, but Mike always felt like he was more Big Brother than a big brother. He didn't understand anything. He was a cop, 24/7. Mike always felt like a criminal, though Steve forgave him again and again -- but that only served to reinforce Mike's feelings of failure. Steve was so patient! It was insulting. He obviously didn't care about him or he would have whopped him.

As much as Mike was secretly impressed with the uniform and how his brother handled himself, Mike wanted nothing to do with police work. He'd been on the other side of the law too many times. He hated cops. Or, any kind of authority. It wasn't because he hated them, really, it's just that they had power and he had none.

Even though Dave didn't leave town right away, he had to get ready for college, so he still had no time for "paling" around with Mike, Moocher and Cyril. Dave took a quick trip to Italy before school began to meet the people he would race with, and he got to spend three weeks with the team. He was so happy, and he deserved it, but it just made Mike more depressed. Next year, in the summer, Dave would be in Italy. Mike wouldn't be anywhere. He'd be in Bloomington. Doing nothing.

Even worse, Dave had a new girlfriend, an exchange student from France, and she was a college girl. Now, instead of an Italian, Dave was French. At least, until he talked about his job possibility. Then Dave was Italian again. But most of the time, in Bloomington with Joelle, he was French instead of Italian. Mike didn't speak those languages. He wasn't all that good at English.

Mike couldn't get a college girl. If he met one, he'd know he wasn't good enough for her, and he didn't have any money to take her anywhere anyway. It would only be a matter of time before she'd throw him over for some "frat" guy. All Mike saw was... nothing. He used to be the cool quarterback, and now his "team" was deserting him and he was left with nothing. His car wasn't even dependable.

It took a few months for Mike to wallow in the trough of depression, before he accepted the fact that he had no choice but to go his own way, to figure out what to do all by himself. He couldn't live in his brother's basement forever, besides, it was cold down there! He couldn't do all that Italian stuff -- and he didn't want to, either!

Well, okay, if he was truthful, he would love to have gone with Dave, but that wasn't going to happen and it wasn't his thing anyway. As much as he would love to have gone to college and joined the football team, he knew he was through with hours of sitting in some class, listening to people drone on and on about stuff they might know about, but meant nothing to Mike. He even checked into jobs at the quarry. They said they might be hiring soon, but right now there was nothing.

"We'd love to hire a home town boy," they had said, "but, fact is, we just don't have the call for stone that we once had. Some of the boys are getting near retirement, but no one has put in for it, and it looks like it will be a while before that happens. We'll be glad to give you a call..."

But Mike knew they would never call. He had a reputation around town, and it wasn't good. The A&P wouldn't take him back, and all those god damn college kids took all the good jobs. Mike could only drive and drive around in his battered old car, taking odd jobs that popped up so he could at least keep gas in his car. The jobs were usually lifting things -- he was trying to keep in shape, no matter what for -- missing his "brothers" and waiting for something to happen, to give him an idea what he should do with his life. He wanted respect. He didn't really want to be a screw-up, but he had nothing else. People respected a strong man, and that's what he wanted to be, someone people respected for his strength. He knew he had that. That was all he had.

Mike thought of going to church, but he just didn't see why he should. He went to church one time and sat in the pews. It felt comforting, but he didn't see as how it would get him anywhere.

If nothing else, he at least wanted to stay in shape, so he lifted weights for a few months and filled out in a way that made girls look twice -- even three times. That felt good, but he didn't dare ask anyone out, as much as he wanted to. He had no money, so he couldn't go to bars, or anywhere else. He was lucky his brother didn't kick him out, but Steve felt he owed it to their parents to let Mike stay and hope he would figure out how life worked. The constant verbal fights were no good. His brother just didn't understand. His "brothers" understood, but they couldn't help him -- besides he was too proud to ask. The only place he felt good was at the gym, where he could see himself in control of SOMETHING -- weights. He wouldn't even have that without his brother's family membership. The loads were increasing and he was getting built! It was a great addiction. He knew that he'd be ready. Ready for what? It didn't matter. There WAS nothing else.

His car was a pile of junk - but his own body was GREAT! Now if he could only figure out how to make a living from it. Competitive body building? He thought about that often as he preened in the mirror, imitating all those guys he saw on the covers of magazines. He wasn't near that big yet, but hey, it was just a matter of time, and this was something he could DO! But, as attractive as that seemed, Mike knew that many people saw those top muscle guys as freaks.

They had to have all their clothes custom made, nothing would fit those bodies. His own clothes were getting tight and now he was having to take his brothers cast-offs to wear decent stuff. Mike couldn't afford to buy anything cool. Or anything at all. Besides, the career of a body builder didn't offer the future Mike had in mind. He wanted respect of everyone, not just some people in a niche sport, no matter what it had done for Arnold Schwarzenegger. Mike didn't want to marry a Kennedy or be a Governor. He just wanted respect.

One day he read about how much supplements could help. He watched a few of the guys take stuff that felt pretty good when he tried it, but he couldn't buy any of that stuff -- that required money too, once they gave you some for free -- just enough to get you addicted. He didn't mind helping Moocher work on his house, but he couldn't tolerate being a moocher himself.

When he found out about "shrinkage" from drugs used by top body building competitors, any drive to go that route evaporated.

But he still loved the way he looked in the mirror. So how could he get respect for looking so good? How could he get MONEY? He saw the movie "American Gigolo", with Richard Gere. That looked like a good idea. Until the end of the movie. Then he just saw another dead end.

One day at the gym, one of the other lifters kept watching Mike, kept looking at him repeatedly. At first, Mike thought the guy was impressed with the amount of weight he could lift, and raised the limits to show off. But then he saw that the other guy could lift a lot more. He was older, VERY fit, and very well groomed. It looked like he had an old, battered "US Marines" t-shirt on.

You can get those at the Goodwill, Mike thought. the guy probably wants to look tough so he can put the "make" on young guys. He'd read about those kinds in the Enquirer. Sleazy bastards! It started to make Mike feel uneasy. He was no queer, he didn't care how much money he might get. He might need to beat somebody up if anyone made a move on him. He tensed and waited a little, trying to focus on his lifts, hoping the guy would stop looking at him, finish up, and LEAVE, but then he couldn't take it any more.

"What are YOU lookin' at?" Mike finally challenged. "You queer or something?" he almost shouted. He looked around, embarrassed that his voice had carried so far. Fortunately it was early in the day and not very many people were there yet. The man started to laugh, which infuriated Mike even more.

"Shut up and get out of here!" Mike screeched, lunging at him in a panic. With the queer now laughing at him, he couldn't take the humiliation. Couldn't he get some respect from ANYONE?

As he lunged at the guy. He intended to show him what he thought about queers, but before he could think it through, the guy grabbed his arm and easily pinned him, as gently as a wrestler can pin a weaker competitor. Oh my god, pinned by a queer! How humiliating! Mike almost cried, but he held on to his tears. He was going to KILL this bastard once he got loose!

"Hold up there, I'm sorry, I'm sorry... listen a minute!" the queer backed down, relieving his grip a little, but still pinning him. "I didn't mean to upset you! Listen to me -- hold up!" He let go of Mike, moving back quickly, hands raised. He allowed Mike plenty of room, plainly not wanting a fight. That was better. Okay, a little respect. Mike could tell this guy what he thought of him without having to punch him.

Mike rubbed the arm that had just been imprisoned. While he had had enough fights to feel he could take a queer easy, this guy was in good shape, and Mike hadn't been fighting lately, so this caught him off guard. How could the queer pin him that fast and that easily? Or maybe the guy just knew things Mike didn't know, things about handling himself in a fight.

"Hey, I'm really sorry, I didn't mean to upset you, let me explain..." the other guy said.

"Don't come any closer or there's gonna be trouble!", Mike warned as he leaned back into his machine, giving the queer a threatening look.

"Hey, I just was watching your technique and your dedication. I was admiring your concentration. You don't let anything bother you when you're lifting, do you?"

"Nothing but a dumb-ass queer!" Mike almost spit on him, but wondered what he would say next. Why was he interested in him? Right here in public? Didn't the guy have any shame?

"You've got this all wrong. Look I'm a recruiter with the Marine Corps. I've been a recruiter for the last 8 years, and we're always looking for guys who are in good shape and can handle themselves. You have a good way about you, tough, but with purpose. Have you ever thought about joining the Corps?"

Now Mike was really thrown by this BIG shift in thought. He was stupified, totally unable to even think of a response, the "reality shift" was so great. The Marine Corps? Him? Well, it had crossed his mind, sure, he'd seen the billboards, but he didn't figure they'd want him considering all the times he'd gotten into trouble at school. His grades were not that great, he'd flunked a bunch of classes, he was barely able to keep his grades up to stay on the football team. If he hadn't been so talented at hitting his receiver, the coach would have dumped him for sure. Ever since his parents died, it was hard to think much about a future with the kind of honor and respect he wanted. He definitely wasn't one of the "Few Good Men". Those posters didn't apply to him. He'd be lucky to get into the Army. He understood all you had to do for that is be breathing. He was breathing, so he figured he'd qualify. But even then, his past would come out, so he didn't even try. What was the use? He was worthless.

"I thought about it." he said, lying, because he was interested that someone was interested in him. "I probably can't qualify." he said, lowering his gaze in embarrassment. Wait until this guy found out about all the stuff he'd done. He didn't even want to go through thinking about the humiliation of being exposed as a stupid, do-nothing troublemaker who couldn't even get into college in his own home town. A nothing. A nobody. A man with NO plan. No money, no abilities, no future. He was at risk of falling into another deep depression when the man reached into his pocket...

I knew he was queer! Mike thought, he's going to give me his phone number and tell me to call him for dinner. Maybe I'll eat, then punch his lights out and split!

But instead, the man pulled out an official looking card with his name, "Henry Johnson, USMC", and a marine saluting on it. Okay, maybe he was legit. Mike reached forward, with caution, still believing this was some sort of come-on. He took it, since he had nothing to lose.

"Our office is in the Mall, do you know where that is?"

"I've seen it... I'll try to get by one of these days." Mike said, not committing himself to anything. He was still surprised to get an invitation, and horrified that he might have to face the fact that he would not measure up.

"Okay, you think about it." Henry said as Mike moved away. "Come on in and let's talk about it. It won't cost you anything."

Mike was so surprised at this unexpected meeting, he cut his workout short, grabbed his gear and left. Was this guy for real or did he just peg Mike for a sucker? He'd have to think about this.

Mike drove around town for over an hour, finally driving by the recruiting office. He was scared and excited at the same time. The Marines. "A Few Good Men"? Was he good enough to make it? No, he thought. You're a nothing, a nobody. You don't know how to do any of those things. He couldn't take humiliation and he knew boot camp would be tough. If, by some quirk or mistake, someone got him signed up, he couldn't get out without prison or some horrible thing happening. The more he thought about it, the scarier it was. He couldn't talk to the guys - if he could even get them to talk about anything. They were all too busy for him now. He used to be the leader, but now he was nothing.

As the days went by, Mike kept up his workouts, but he didn't run into Henry until a week later.

"Hey, I thought you were coming by!" Henry prompted.

"I thought about it, but I decided I like it right here in Bloomington." he said with great assurance. "I decided against it." He threw on more weights to show Henry he wasn't afraid.

Henry had run into lots of guys thinking all sorts of of thoughts about the Corps, and what he knew is that, usually, they had NO idea what it was really about. They looked at some part of the service, or saw some movie, and thought they knew it all, when really, it's a very large and comprehensive job path where many different types of people found their life's calling, in many different ways. Sometimes they stayed in, and sometimes they didn't, but Henry always believed that their lives were better for having joined and learning the discipline that goes with it. Especially guys with attitude -- and this guy clearly had attitude. He believed he did every young man a big favor by at least explaining away pre-conceived notions and making sure he really understood the opportunity. And this young man looked like he needed to learn about some new opportunities. Sometimes these guys with low self esteem made the best Marines. They find the home and the pride they need.

"Well, tell ya what. Come by and let me explain the possibilities to you. No obligation, you don't need to sign anything, it's not like school. You're your own man, and if you decide it's not for you, we shake hands and you go home. Fair enough?" You call me ahead of time, I'll even have pizza waiting. You know I'll bug you until you at least let me explain the possibilities"

Mike couldn't think of a good response. Lord knows he needed possibilities. Free food was a nice thought. He knew the recruiting center was legit. Sure, free food sounded good. At least he could eat ONE meal that his brother wouldn't be able to hold over his head.

"Okay, I'll come by tomorrow. Will you be there?"

"Come by this afternoon, how about 4 o'clock? Don't be scared."

"Scared? I'm not scared!" Mike protested, again a little too loud.

Now Mike felt trapped, like his honor was on the line. He didn't want this guy to think he was chicken. He wasn't afraid of being a soldier, especially now that Vietnam was done. He'd watched that war, and was glad he didn't have to think about that.

"Okay, I'll be there at 4." He now felt the obligation, since he knew that if he didn't go, he'd just have to face Henry in the gym a few days later. Might as well get it over with. He'd listen politely, eat the pizza, then go home, and it would be DONE. This guy would realize that Mike had nothing to offer the Corps and he'd leave him alone. Mike couldn't feel any worse about himself, he'd still feel like crap, but at least his stomach would be full!

"Okay! I'll call for a pizza delivery at 4 o'clock." Henry said happily. "See you then!" He'd get another chance to explain the best about his experience and maybe he'd have another "taker". He viewed his work with missionary zeal. Why, anyone would want to join -- if they just understood!

Mike had to drive around a few times before he had the nerve to actually go in, but from the moment he stepped into the Marine Corps recruiting office, it was a done deal. The posters, the flyers, the sales pitch -- and this Henry guy seemed to really know what he was talking about. He didn't seem to see anything about Mike's past to disqualify him. Mike suddenly felt the attraction of authority. HE could be that authority -- he could be the quarterback again! -- maybe. That was a VERY appealing thought.

When Mike told Henry his name, he got a surprise.

"Really? Are you the Mike Kozlowski that was on the Little 500 team that won?"

"Yeah, I was on the team." Mike said, hoping that Henry wouldn't realize that he ONLY jumped on the bike to help Dave and had hardly done any of the race.

"Well hell, son, you saved the whole damn day! If it wasn't for you, that team wouldn't have had a chance! I saw that race, and the other guys were out of it. It was only you taking up the slack that meant they could win! That fella Dave is a pretty spectacular bike rider, but he couldn't have won without you. You see, son, that's exactly the kind of thing we look for in our Marines, the guys who will put the pedal to the metal when the chips are down, for their brothers, for their team. You have the heart of a Marine, whether you know it or not, before you even sign up!"

Mike's pride began to pull itself out of the gutter. He'd never thought about it that way. It was true, Moocher and Cyril were DONE and Dave wasn't ready to get back on the bike yet, if it wasn't for him, they would have lost, no matter how good a bike rider Dave was. His ears opened to everything else Henry had to say. Mike began to confess that he had a bad past, full of waste and no accomplishments, but Henry seemed to actually <u>like</u> that. He cut Mike short.

"So, you got into a lot of fights? Well don't worry about that, you can fight for your country and get paid for doing it. Your past is your past, Mike. Your future is what you make of it, and the Marines will help you make it your own." Henry said.

As Henry talked on, Mike envisioned what he'd been looking for all his life: discipline and respect for ideals that he could learn, plus, a path that he could actually follow. A brotherhood —

some of the things he loved most about football and his Bloomington "brothers".

As he thought more about it, first, it <u>looked</u> good. He would look great in a Marine uniform right now, he knew that. He identified with a poster in the Marines recruiting office. And, he'd have some money. He could get his teeth taken care of. Second, Henry assured him that he'd have a new beginning. Henry said the Corps didn't care about a guy's past, but focused on his future. He explained all the different jobs Mike could learn, and about possibilities after he got out -- if he decided to get out after his first hitch, and with advanced military training, he could become a cop. A cop! That would surprise his brother. Maybe he could teach his brother a few things! He chuckled at the thought. Henry pointed out that boot camp would be easier for him than for many others because he'd kept in shape. He knew that was true. When Henry described the retirement plan, that seemed like a long way off, but it sounded GREAT. At last he saw the reason he had kept in shape all those days. He was going to be a Marine! ALL of his brothers, natural and adopted, would be so proud!

As much as he hated school for many things, football was so important to him that he had forced himself to study to keep his grades up just high enough to play. Much to his surprise, one day he found himself on the auditorium stage, where someone handed him a diploma. Without football, he may not have graduated, but it got him through, and now that Marine requirement was met too. Mike signed up.

Soon after, Mike FLEW through the physical tests for Corps entry. He easily got top scores in every physical test. He was so glad he hadn't started smoking again! Once in the Corps, Mike didn't like the discipline required any more than he did any kind of discipline, but he knew, first and foremost, that the military required regimentation, as a "given". Of course he'd follow orders -- that's what military discipline was all about. If he learned how to conduct himself, he knew that the military would give him the skills and ability to move up the ladder and increase his self-respect. At some point, he'd expect his orders to be obeyed too. When his brother tried to get him to follow rules, those were just his brother's rules, so he often defied them, though now he realized that his brother had really been right. These military rules were the same for everyone. He'd watched enough military shows on TV enough to realize how important discipline was to being ready for foreign service, which he fully expected might save his life some day. It was a little rough learning the rules initially, but once he got into it, he figured out how to do things and became increasingly comfortable with what was required. After a while it was second nature -- plus, he knew trying to argue with a superior officer was ridiculous. His plan was to become the superior officer, so he'd better figure out what that meant and what was needed.

Broken Reverie

Suddenly, Mike's reverie was broken by some shouts to his left. He turned to look at the action. The last 20 years had gone by in such a flash. And now he was at a bike race, watching his little girl -- his little girl who seemed to have a lot of speed in her legs! -- race on the velodrome. He was so proud! He looked around to see if he could pick any of his "brothers" out of the crowd.

Mike looked around the track, then he saw a tall man with curly hair lumber across the other side of the track with a girl who also had masses of curls. He knew the hair and height so well, he wondered if that was Cyril or if is was just a Cyril "look-alike". A few minutes later Mike watched another tall, lanky man approach the tall, curly haired man, greetings exchanged, then the hug. The other man had to be Dave, of course he would have on a cycling cap and stylish bike clothes. Mike was excited to see this exchange, but didn't know what to do. He couldn't cross the track. He had never spent much time around tracks, and knew little about how things worked. Maybe by the time Moocher got here, he could find a way to cross the track, or maybe walk back around and find his wife or Nancy, who were sitting near the announcer's stand. He was sure that that was Moocher's kid he'd seen at registration, and now he saw him on the infield of the track.

It was all coming together. Uncharacteristically, Mike felt shy. This was not a place where he felt at home. It was foreign territory. Would they remember him? Well, of course, they'd remember him, but would their relationship have changed over these years? It had been a long time.

2. Dave

Dave waited, excited about the prospect of seeing his brothers after all these years. He watched the familiar ritual of unloading equipment and setting up "camp" in places around the track. It was so familiar and he loved it now as he always did. It had been a long time since that day in Bloomington.

Once he won the Little 500, Dave got a huge surge of respect, both within himself and from unexpected sources. The Italian racers who crashed Dave during the CinZano Road Race had stayed in Bloomington to do some business and to watch this "Little 500" they had heard about, an unusual yearly race among college students. They didn't have this sort of thing in Italy, so they were curious. They were surprised when they realized that the young upstart they thought had jumped in their race as a cheater a few days before turned out to be a local champion they didn't know about. They hadn't noticed him at the starting line. All US riders looked the same to them that day. They hadn't believed any rider in the U.S. could keep up with the big, powerhouse Italian team. But when they watched the Little 500, they knew they had made a grave mistake, insulting all they held dear and noble in bike racing: EARNING your victory. They realized that they themselves hadn't earned their victory that day in the road race as cleanly as they thought. They thought they had dealt with a race "crasher" who joined them several miles down the road -- after all, how could some small town American rider HOPE to keep up with the powerful CinZano professional team? -- but instead they now realized that they had fouled a talented rider by sticking a pump in his front wheel and causing him to crash. They hadn't realized!

Roberto, the rider who stuck his pump into Dave's wheel, called to apologize to him a few days after the "Cutters" won the 500. He could not say "Scuse, scuse, scuse!" (apologies!) enough times.

"We din see you at the start of CinZano" Roberto explained, "We thought you was race crasher. We thought you jump in half way through the race, and cheat! Our rule: "crasher" gets crashed. I'm sorry, we didn't realize you are Champion until we saw "Little 500".

They had run into many race crashers over their many races, especially in a place like America, where people didn't take cycling as seriously as in Italy. They saw it as their duty to crash someone who jumped in half way through the race, trying to act like they could keep up with the international powerhouse CinZano riders. They trained for many years to race at their high level, and had no respect for cheaters. Once they saw the "500" and read the newspapers, they realized their mistake and wanted to make it up to Dave by offering him a job. Besides, he could help the team.

"We see you are REAL champion," Roberto said, "... we have highest respect for man who show strength and heart. We regret not let you ride with us at CinZano race. At least we would let you pull!" He let out a bawdy laugh.

"But job offer is real. We see how much you love Italy and riding and we want you to come with us, be with us." Roberto persisted.

Dave's heart almost stopped when he got this call. There was nothing in the world he could want more than racing with the Italians. College? What's that? Racing or race support, he didn't care, as long as he could be with The Italians - he'd learn so much! And, his Italian would improve so much! Maybe he'd even learn how to cook! If he could ride with them, at their level...

"Che Bello!" Dave exclaimed, "My best dream! There is nothing I want more!"

"But wait", he stopped. "I promised my mother and father I would go to college after the 500. It's all set up." He was quiet for a few seconds. "I may need to say no. You have no idea how hard this is to say to you, Roberto."

But Roberto didn't hesitate.

"Nessun problema - no problem!" Roberto replied. "Promise to mother and father should never break. You are young. You can work our race whenever you come, summer maybe? You can ride with us and learn. You finish college, you ride. You decide, you let us know. We love people who love bicycles and Italy with us. Bellissimo! Here is phone number. You call when you want come work. Hard work, but you young, you learn."

"Deal! As soon as I know my schedule, I'll call." shouted Dave. His heart was full! His family now extended to Italy! As much as he hated to leave his brothers, The Cutters team of Mike, Cyril, Moocher and himself, he looked at this opportunity as simply expanding this family. After all, Italians love large families!

Over the next few years, college was interspersed with riding and Dave lived his dream. Mom and dad even came on a couple of trips. Life was good!

The only thing Dave really missed was his Bloomington brothers -- the "Cutters", the "B-Town" boys. He didn't really want to go his own way. He imagined taking them with him -- have Mike drive the chase car, Cyril help him plot strategy and prime wins! -- and Moocher could come if he wanted, he would be a great wheel builder. But Dave already knew Moocher was too involved with Nancy to leave the States. It was here that his fantasy bike support team came apart. It was time for them to go their own ways. As much as he hated to admit it, it was the truth. That's okay, they'd write -- or at least, Nancy would. Moocher wasn't good at writing, but Nancy was. Dave already knew that as a new rider, his desire to haul his B-Town friends along would have to wait until later. Knowledge of bike mechanics takes a while to learn, a lot tougher than people think, so it would take Moocher a while to learn. If Mike drove the chase car, he might get mad and cause accidents. No, Dave would have to go by himself. But he promised himself that ONE DAY, one FINE day, they'd all get together for another bike event, even if only as spectators. He never forgot that promise to himself in his heart and in his intent, to the other guys. Now the happy day had come, he thought. He hoped he'd see them all at this great event, the Grand Prix in Seattle.

The Infield

Dave settled down in the infield to wait for Joslyn, his very own bike racing daughter. He sat under an umbrella on this gorgeous day, just watching riders cross the track and set up with gear and teams. He watched for the others.

Some teams had great equipment, very flashy, and great team uniforms, all covered with sponsors, and that meant MONEY. Bicycling was expensive, even on the track, the simplest form of bike racing. Dave was fortunate to have enjoyed considerable wealth due to his job and language talents, plus having team connections. He had facilitated many a business meeting, making deals of great profitability for his company and he had gotten the bonuses that rewarded his quick wit and positive outlook. Too bad he invested in that vineyard in Napa and he was in danger of losing that, but that's okay, he still had plans and enough money and connections for other dreams to stay happy in life. He just didn't know how to tell the family of his financial troubles. But, he'd have to worry about that later. Not today. Dave got up, and exited the track to get "his girl". She should have arrived by now.

"Come on, Joslyn" he called, "grab your track bike, I'll grab your road bike and the rest of your gear. We can come back and get the food and blankets later." She was standing in a group of riders, chatting and laughing. You'd think she didn't have a race coming up! But he could see that she partly was chatting to distract herself from her own nervousness.

Dave hoisted the road bike and the rest of the gear on his shoulder. Joslyn was still gathering her track bike, her wheels, and the rest of her stuff. They'd need to make another trip for her rollers. He'd wait for her at the gate. This road bike felt so good. It was so much lighter than the bikes he used to ride, even the super-light bikes the Italians gave him back when he rode with the CinZano team. It was light as a feather. Her track bike was even lighter.

Those were old racing days were great days and he knew that later in life Joslyn would see these as great days with memories of great friendships as he did. Bicycling did that to you.

The summer when Dave raced in his first Tour de France, his college friend Joelle was home in France for the summer, working some of the races. Though they had dated in Bloomington, school required a lot of work, so they never had as much time for fun activities as they wanted. They had planned to meet that summer, but also ran into each other unexpectedly. At one event, she was one of the "kiss girls", as fans called them. There were lots of "Tour hostesses", or "podium girls". Their job was to kiss race winners (French style, on one cheek, then the other) when the winners received their flowers and medals or trophies and look pretty for the cameras. Sometimes they were related to race sponsors or got the job for some "fun" reason, though these days the job was more of an official capacity.

When Dave ran into Joelle, it was at a race stop in Bordeaux. Her uncle was one of the race sponsors, a partner in a Bordeaux wine company that Dave particularly liked. When he learned she was a relative, she became particularly memorable and not just some college girl he dated. She knew a lot about wine, and gave Dave a tour of the vineyard. He was fascinated, not only by her, but about her knowledge of grapes and farming grapes for wine. She hadn't been in a position to show that knowledge off before, since they don't have vineyards in Bloomington. They became closer that summer when they had more free time. She was teaching Dave more French every day -- including some terms that are not common to French classes. He was pretty good at German and Spanish, too, but not quite as good as French and Italian. It was this first summer when he began seeing her as his future wife.

Joelle had grown up with great wines, but Dave had a lot to learn. While racing throughout Europe, he worked at becoming an aficionado of great wines, and could almost -- not quite, yet, but he was hopeful -- tell you what vineyard a certain wine came from. He prided himself on this fine-tuned skill, which most people didn't have an opportunity to develop. One thing you could say about Dave: he was always trying to improve himself. Plus, he had a knack with people. Over the years, he charmed both men and women. Everyone loved him.

Dave went to Italy (and France) every summer until he graduated and then went to work for CinZano full time. He loved the racing and the traveling. Every year was a new adventure of hope as the team made plans and he learned all the behind-the-scenes lessons and intrigues of a professional team. As much as he loved it, CinZano saw another future for him after eight years of full-time racing. He had a facility for languages and became fluent in Italian and French.

CinZano called on him to be their spokesman for a wide variety of issues, racing and business, and after the years of professional racing,

Dave saw that he was needed in other areas of the company. A bike racer is always a bike racer, so Dave never gave it up, but he moved to handling bicycle events and associated responsibilities when he and Joelle got married. Sure, he could race and start a family, but he wanted more, so he settled into business.

Dave had a special talent that endeared him to CinZano. It went like this: There were times when Dave realized that a deal he had in play could quickly evaporate if he translated exactly what the speaker said, without such subtle changes as better word choice, vocal inflection, and facial expression, to maintain good will. Dave's sensitivity to the disadvantaged, both the boys he loved and his own dad, allowed him to interact in such a way as to maintain the feeling of respect that the less advantaged person might need in strategic meetings to successfully be persuaded to take a deal that otherwise might be rejected. It was a very special talent.

Dave understood people -- and he liked them -- that was his greatest gift. He once gave his dad a trophy he had won because he realized that dad was feeling left out of the adventure and the happiness. He learned a lot about the "why"s when he and his dad started having REAL talks, after dad's heart attack. Imagining life without his father gave Dave a deep appreciation of his dad's struggles in life and his pride in stonecutting that was now a lost art. Everyone has pride in some aspect of themselves, and if that pride can be tapped, it can make life better for everyone involved. Dave awarded "trophies" to all of his clients and employers alike, whether it was an exceptionally wonderful bottle of wine, some rare cheese, or a smile and a handshake at the right time. There were so many ways to give, and Dave knew when his special talent was needed. It paid handsomely too, which didn't hurt.

In the mid-80s, CinZano began moving into a new business model, eventually morphing into other companies until it no longer resembled the family owned company to which Dave was particularly attached. As devoted at he was to CinZano, eventually he moved to Constellation Brands. This company allowed Dave to sample the best wines in the world, a rare privilege for a young man from Indiana.

Track racing was something Dave had tried during his European years, especially racing 6-Day races in Belgium and Holland, which he adored. The roar of the crowds, the challenge... ! His wife Joelle was a track enthusiast, since her uncle had also raced track in the old days.

She'd grown up hearing about it. But, a guy can only be so many places to race at one time, so Dave hadn't spent time on tracks with the same dedication as he did the roads. He knew that "ride the track" feeling, quite different from road racing, and was happy their daughter Joslyn took to track racing so he could enjoy her success vicariously and see all of her races take place right before his eyes.

It had been a while since Dave had been in the States, even though he had an investment in the Napa vineyard. He'd been traveling so long, every place looked like home, but he'd been to Seattle so many times, he'd grown very fond of this Northwest area, too. It was special.

Dave looked over at the next tent, where a young man was working on his bike. The kid didn't have any of his own tools, but no one seemed to mind his borrowing theirs. He was blazingly quick, tightening his wheels, inflating his tires, knocking, thumping, checking, to make sure everything felt and sounded like it should. He couldn't wait to get on the track, that was plain. But every time someone needed a check or some adjustment, he'd oblige with no objection. In fact, he looked like he was happy to help anyone and everyone who asked.

One boy called him "Chilly", filling Dave with interest. That must be Moocher's boy. The boy turned around and Dave could see Moocher and Nancy in his face. He could also see his excitement at preparing for the race, jumping on his bike without his helmet.

"Helmet!" shouted Dave.

Chilly looked around, first at Dave, then at his helmet, then, throwing the helmet on, shouting back.

"Thanks Mister!", pedaling happily away, toward the track for warm-up. He joined other riders there, some he knew, some he didn't.

Dave thought Chilly might recognize him, but he could see that all he was focused on was racing. He knew that feeling. He was always like that, especially when he looked forward to a good race. On the track, the world evaporated into riding fast and the lovely feel of centrifugal force, especially when hitting the turns and moving left on the slant. He could still feel it, even just sitting in this chair. The lovely rhythm... Dave closed his eyes in reverie, happily enjoying the warm sun.

Joslyn

Like her dad, Joslyn loved the distance races, Points, Scratch, Madison, she even tried a Pursuit once in a while, just to see how well she could do. That was so satisfying, it changed her focus to track. She still raced on the road, but that had become only to build endurance for track racing. In truth, Joslyn liked the fact that she had a captive audience in track racing. In road racing, the peloton goes by and you may not see them again during the whole race, or, if you're lucky, you may see them in a hour or so. In track racing, no one needs to leave the track to eat dinner. You can buy it from the food wagon on the side of the track in the food area, so spectators can be there all the time. Joslyn felt they could watch HER! She loved the social-ness of it, plus being able to see all the guys racing. She always had an eye out for cute guys and there were plenty of them in lycra.

Dave loved watching Joslyn take on all other women in the Points race. She was good at distance, just give her enough miles and she could beat anyone, Dave thought, but this was a little different. Now she was on a track and the race was 60 laps of a 400 meter track. Dave recalled the days when the women just "sat in", riding slow and waiting for the sprint. Sometimes he felt thoroughly embarrassed for them, they rode so slow, it wasn't even a race. It was more like sit on your bike and hope you have a sprint. In those days, there were frequent accidents because some girls had hardly ridden a track before and didn't now how to ride in a close pack like on a track. His own group of men SCREAMED around the track in Points races, so fast, each rider had only a millisecond to decide where to go or whose wheel would get you the most points, especially if you could sprint around him at the last minute. Ahhhh those were the days.

But now, the women's races were as competitive as the men. With better coaching and competition, especially since the women's purses were raised so they were often fully comparable to the men, the women's field was exploding. Dave could hardly believe how different it was now for his little girl.

She loved riding, but never seemed to want to push through that "barrier of pain" that he felt was required if she wanted to win. They had that conversation a couple of years ago.

"Hey, dad, it hurt too much, so I backed off!" especially when it came to the 3000 meter time trial, also known as the Pursuit. She was really good at watching her coach and keeping track of her splits, but she just refused to work so hard that she threw up at the end of the effort. Shoot, throwing up was the proof you'd done all you were physically capable of doing, which told Dave she had NOT gone all out! He used to push her, letting her know about those somewhat unpleasant "secrets of champions" that the "common folk" don't see, as to how far you need to push to be a champion, but she simply said:

"Then I don't want to be a champion. I'm fine just riding my bike! I love riding my bike, dad, don't make it an unpleasant chore or I won't do it at all!" He knew she was lying about that last part, but she made her point.

Dave's dad was sitting nearby during this conversation and butted in with his opinion, as usual.

"You know all those times I tried to get you to STOP riding your bike, Dave? Remember when I told you you couldn't go to the Italian race? Remember what response that got for me?'"

"Yeah... " said Dave, tentatively.

"You never stopped! You worked ever harder! You did it to spite me. You were never "too tired" no matter how much I tried to wear you out. Kids will do the OPPOSITE of whatever you try to make them do, so my advice to you, something I learned the hard way, is if you want her to do something, tell her you want her to do the opposite. That'll work!"

Dave chuckled. Joslyn was nearby, but concentrating on her equipment, so he didn't think she had heard grandpa's advice. Dad was right, that would probably work. He'd try it...

"I hate to admit, that you're right." Dave dropped his eyes. "One of the reasons I threw myself into it double-hard is because you tried to stop me. I never felt so good and free as when I was riding and you said "NO!" I get it."

Turning to Joslyn, Dave said: "Okay, I'll tell you what. I'll be here, ready to give you support whenever you need it, but otherwise, you can ask the advice of anyone you want. I'm glad you have a couple of other coaches, so between all of us, you might be able to figure out what's best for you and do that."

"No problem, Dad, I know you have all the goods, I won't forget where the "source" is located. Meanwhile, I'm going to have FUN and ride my bike!"

Dave watched her saunter away happily, mounting her bike and continuing the warmup she had started on her rollers. He watched her on the track, looking like she had everything under control on each lap. She knew where to be and whose wheel to get on. She had that "full of happiness" look that he loved to see on her face and in her eyes.

Whenever he saw that, he no longer cared what place she took. His little girl was HAPPY. Nothing else beat that. Maybe she'd get on the awards stand and she'd be happier still, if that were possible. But it didn't matter. If it didn't matter to her, it shouldn't matter to him.

Dave knew that, included in her happiness at this particular event. was flirting with the boys, but there was nothing he could do about that. She was a romantic, like her dad. And, after all, her mother was French, one of the "romance" countries. She might be just showing off for some kid -- he could never keep track of which one -- but if it helped her win, and it seemed to, that was fine. Remembering what his dad said, she'd probably run off with one of them if he tried to stop the flirting. It was part of her inspiration to flirt, especially on or before a ride. He knew that one boy here was of particular interest to her, some kid with a Mohawk and green hair -- disgusting, but what could he do about it? (How did the kid get his helmet on that hair-do?) He guessed he was getting old. The kid was a hot rider, one of the best, and he had lots of girls vying for his attentions, so maybe Joslyn would just get lost in the crowd. He hoped.

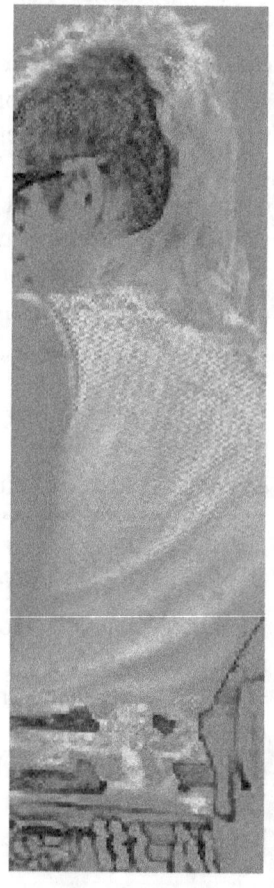

Meanwhile, Dave walked over to where a proud grandpa watched his favorite granddaughter compete in a very exciting bike race. Mr Stohler had become a regular fixture at the Little 500 ever since his son won it. His son won it all by himself, if you heard him tell it, though then he'd go on and on about the other boys and how Dave never could have done it without them. The interesting thing was, if you saw the race, it was all true! He loved those boys, just as though they were his own kids. Moocher was the one he still saw around town, him and his five kids. He never could have predicted Moocher would do so well for himself, back in the old days. Many times Mooch would come to dinner and hang around the Stohler house, just because he was lonely and had no one to help him. Poor kid. Mr Stohler saw ads for helping orphans in foreign countries, but he knew a kid right in Bloomington who needed help and he was perfectly happy to help him. He sort of took it on as his personal mission.

Once Mooch and Nancy got married, he'd loan them tools and once in a while he'd go help or just sit and watch Mike and Moocher work on the old house. Lord knows there was a lot to do, Mr Stohler wondered how it could even still stand up, but apparently the foundation was good, so they just kept worked along. Dave was gone, and even though dad had a brand new young daughter of his own in the house, sometimes it was just nice to get away. He had mellowed a lot since his heart attack, and his doctor said it would be good for him to take the walk to Moocher's, visit, then walk home. Moocher would fix some tea and cookies were always available, so it was pretty nice. Moocher would limit him to two small cookies, but he didn't mind, he knew it was his way of showing love. He didn't know anyone more respectful than Moocher, who was thrilled to have a father figure, since his own seemed gone forever.

His attention reverted to the Points race that had just started. He'd heard the gun, but now he was aware that the race had actually begun. Last he looked, the riders were lined up at the rail -- then they needed to come around one lap together before the gun signaled the start of the race. He had sort of registered it, but now the points were actually accumulating, so he paid more attention. Plus, his granddaughter was winning some!

"Come on, Joslyn!" Dave shouted as he ambled toward his dad.

Dave watched Joslyn come around for two more points. She didn't win the lap, but she added points, and he knew that she'd feel happy about that. He saw the boy with the green mohawk watching her -- or was he watching all the girls? He couldn't tell. He assumed it was Joslyn, with a father's pride.

Well, he'd better just sit down and have that chat dad seemed to want to have while the race went on. It would be a while before the points would accumulate enough so that he'd have reason to get excited. He approached Angelina, his sister, who was sitting with his dad. Of course they had chosen an Italian name for her. Italian families stick together. His dad always said:

"But Evelyn, we are NOT Italian!" But he knew who had won that fight by the name his sister carried. He liked the name "Angelina".

"Hi Angie" Dave smiled, happy to see his sister again.

"Hi, Big Bro! I'm so glad you're here, me and the kids want to go get ice cream! Take all the time you want, I know dad's been wanting to talk to you ever since he got here. See you for dinner!"

She walked away, her two daughters in tow, great kids.

Dave bent down, kissing his dad on one cheek, then the other.

"Papa! I'm so glad to see you!"

"I'm glad to see you too, son, even if you do need to give me those froggy kisses." dad said, wincing, but with more pleasure than distress.

"Old habits, dad. If you lived in Europe, you'd get them all the time, even from compete strangers!" Dave exclaimed.

"That's another reason you give me for not going out of the country, aside from my lumbago." He shifted in his chair.

"Lumbago? Do you have lumbago, Papa?"

"Just an expression of speech for getting old. Lots of things start to ache and you don't know what they are, so you just call them lumbago. I always thought that described it well enough. Fact is, I'm just glad to be here." he confessed. "Speaking of which, we need to talk about something that you don't want to talk about, but I'm your father, and that's what fathers do."

"What, dad, do you need something? Is mom okay? Is Angie and her family doing alright? You know I'll want to help."

"I know you will, son. That's what we need to talk about. Now look, I don't want you to get mad or feel insulted or any of that stuff. If I could help you, I'd offer, but I just want to understand what has happened."

"Sure, dad, I'll tell you anything you want to know. You know I don't hide things from you."

"Okay, then tell me about the vineyard."

The Vineyard...

"What do you mean, you've been there, you know what it's like, it's beautiful there, one of the most beautiful spots on earth."

"Yes, so tell me what's happened with it." Mr Stohler looked at Dave in the eyes. Dave dropped his eyes.

"Well gosh, dad, I hope you can come out again this year, harvest is coming up, and you know what a great time that is." said Dave, eyes still lowered, looking at the ground, then looking up at him sideways.

"No, I want to know what's happening with it." Mr Stohler persisted.

"Nothing's happening with it." Dave became faintly agitated.

"Look, son, you know I love you. Joelle knows I love you, too, and the last time I had a little chat with her, she started to cry and I made her tell me what's wrong. I wish I could help, but I can't. But I still want to understand what's happened. Are they getting ready to foreclose on it?"

Dave shot up, just as the girls came around. About 20 more laps to go. Dave didn't know exactly where Joslyn stood in points, but from the look on her face, she was doing well and she loved competition.

"Go, Joslyn! Watch the points! Go Joslyn!!" Dave screamed.

She ignored him, of course, partly because she was concentrating on her race and partly because she really couldn't hear much out in a pack of 28 women, all going FAST and trying for points every 5 laps. She sensed dad and grandpa though, like riders might, just for a split second and she knew they were rooting for her.

Dave sat down, realizing that his dad just wanted to understand what happened in one of the saddest events in Dave's life, the impending loss of his precious vineyard. He partly wanted to avoid it because it was just so painful, but even more, it pointed to a casual lack of enjoyment of a property that needed much more in care and commitment than he had been able put into it because he'd been gone so much. He should have known better. Some of it was Dave's fault, some not. All in all, it just made him sad to even think of it, but he summoned up the fortitude to tell dad the whole story. Well, maybe abbreviate it a little bit so dad wouldn't fall asleep with intricate details. He knew that his dad had given up feeling he had to be the tough guy a long time ago. He just wanted to understand.

"Okay, dad, I'll tell you the story. It's not a short one, but I'll try to make it just the facts." Dave settled back in his chair. Dad did the same.

"You just tell it however it comes to you. It's just fact, whatever happened is just what happened." Dad was so great now. The "old cranky guy" within his father still cropped up from time to time, but he seemed to have mellowed with age and security.

"As you know, I bought the vineyard with my partner Al, and neither of us really had enough resources to own a vineyard. I was between jobs and not in a good place, and Al was retired. We bought the place for two million dollars. We each dipped into our resources to come up with a quarter million each. They never should have loaned us the other one and a half million dollars, but we figured they wouldn't have loaned it to us if they didn't think we could pay if off, would they? But in truth, we knew we shouldn't have gotten the loan -- we didn't expect to! We just put it in as a lark! But all of a sudden we had the money. They must have thought we could pay it. Neither us had ever before been loaned money we had trouble paying off. But if we were honest, we knew we shouldn't have taken the loan. We used to joke that if they'd loan to us, they'd loan to anyone! And sadly, that was actually true. We got caught in that banking scam that bilked billions from home owners, and we were part of it. When we first looked at the place, our realtor told us we could have other people do the work on the crops -- you know I'm no farmer -- and we could pay them out of our harvest proceeds. It sounded like good deal, like the vineyard would pay for itself. It turned out to be only a money pit.

Al had a tractor, which saved us some money, and we worked the vineyard ourselves for a couple of years. We couldn't do harvest, so we had to farm that out (so to speak). Harvest was so wonderful, we always loved it! And I tried to be there each year, of possible. We were always able to pay the harvest crew. Al knew enough to bring doughnuts and coffee out to them. Usually they had their own lunches. You remember how fast they were, that time you came to watch the pickers, they were magicians at finding the grapes and cutting them so quickly! I loved watching them.

Meanwhile, since I was gone so much, I let out the rooms to renters. For some reason I still can't figure out, most of the renters we had thought the house was a party house. Married men who rented a room would bring their girlfriends to party with the other roommates. While it was great fun for food and drink, it was shocking when I realized what they were doing. Plus, one of them snuck in a couple of stinky dogs and then tried to ask for a "dog deposit" back that he had never given. All in all, with the exception of a few, the people who rented and left the rooms in the vineyard house were scoundrels, and I was unfortunately not close enough to the property to monitor them. Al had his own problems, with a son in jail and a daughter married to an abusive husband, forcing her to come live in his small house with her kids until

they could set up on their own. You can imagine how that worked out.

Meanwhile, Al kept the tractoring going, which was a great help in the vineyard. We worked together watering, bargaining with the winery who purchased our grapes, trying to keep the 30 year old farm house in order. We replaced windows and rugs, dealt with a flood from housekeepers who loaded and started a dishwasher that turned out not to work, flooding the house. There was SO much to do and it required a full time property manager. I was working hard enough to just pay the taxes of $22,000 a year and all the other expenses, utilities, etc. I knew it was too much for me, but I didn't see much room to move.

First, according to the agreement we signed, we couldn't sell the property for three years without a big penalty. Second, when that hurdle was cleared, and I realized that we would have to sell it, Al refused to even think about selling at less than a price that was completely unobtainable. The fact is, he didn't want to sell it. Third, a movie called "Sideways" came out, wherein the central character declares that he will have "nothing to do with that f***in' Merlot!". Our Merlot price took a huge dump, even though, in fact, it's a great wine -- the best! Fourth, the valley had a dip in grape production -- and so did we. Then there was the corporation next door that put in a well about 30 feet from our well, which seemed to mean that we had less water.

Then, the coup de grace -- the winery didn't pay us our fourth year. Al felt like their buddy and persuaded me that they would. "See? they were always late!" The next year, the same winery didn't pay us again. That was another coup de grace -- but the bull wasn't dead yet! The final segment of this story is even worse."

"Meanwhile, in theory, if a winery doesn't pay you, the grapes remain your property and if they bottle them, for instance, the bottles become yours. Well, nice idea, dad, but it was no where in fact or evidence in Napa Valley. We went to a lawyer and were told we had been doing business with the biggest snakes in the valley in the vineyard that had stiffed us. The biggest fight Al and I ever had was about selling to them the second year. I said "NO!" and should have stuck to my guns. "They always pay" he cajoled. Well, they didn't pay us for those two years. In fact, they declared bankruptcy and ended up paying most suppliers something like .20 cents on the dollar -- if anything -- and only paid us after we harassed them online. Al saw packed bottles of our Chardonnay that the winery didn't seem to know anything about once I got there. The ship was sinking, and between my shrinking bank account and refusal of my partner to see the writing on the wall, we were doomed. But it gets worse, if you can believe that! Wait until you hear this story." He saw Angie stride up.

"Hi!" Angelina said. "Are you two still talking?"

"Yeah, I'm about to tell him the goriest details of all." Dave replied.

"Okay, well, I was just checking. We're going to go root for Joslyn, the race will be finished pretty soon!" and she walked on, girls in tow.

"In desperation, I put up a website, advertising that we might take on another partner. I got a response from a man who sounded like the answer to our prayers. He said he wanted to invest and he had enough money to make it worth our while. As you know, I don't make any moves without legal paperwork in place. Al jumped at the idea, and the new guy, Ed, came to discuss possibilities. We met at the house and he looked everything over and we all talked about ideas for our partnership. It sounded like our savior had arrived! All we needed was a legal agreement. He said he would send paperwork soon and we would be ready to take that paperwork to our lawyers. It seemed like it was set.

The next thing I knew, (I was gone again) our new friend Ed was moved into the house with Al's encouragement. Soon after that he was collecting MY rents, telling the two remaining renters that he was now the boss and he'd be taking care of things. The woman renter contacted me and told me what was going on, but I couldn't return to do anything about it, I was working. Ed seemed to be going nuts, walking around with a chainsaw, cutting down trees on the property that had NO reason to be cut down and threatening my renter, Joyce. I contacted Al and it turned out that Ed had taken over the property, convincing a young man to work for him that he never paid and convincing Al that he and Al could take the property from me and wouldn't have to pay me a dime!

"Dave, how could you let that happen?" dad exclaimed in wonderment.

"Yes, I know, it's unbelievable." said Dave. "I felt so helpless, Al had been a wonderful partner until then. And now he thought he could just take the property without any legal transfers or other legal actions? But dad, it gets unbelievably WORSE STILL!"

"How can it get worse than that?" dad asked.

"Well, it doesn't really get worse for me, because I believed I had legal protection even though I had no money to execute anything. But get this: As part of the "take the vineyard from Dave" plan, Ed helped Al declare bankruptcy. He sat down and helped him fill out the paperwork, credit card and other account numbers and all. Before Al realized it, our Con Man Ed had cleaned out any remaining credit possessed by Al and left him not only in bankruptcy, but as broke as he could possibly be! Furthermore, Al told me our pal Ed owed $10,000 to the young man he had working for him, which was not and would never be paid."

"That is unbelievable! How did you get rid of him, could you have him arrested?" dad asked.

"Even more incredible, this little snippet of the story: Al told me that some men had come to the house who were reportedly from the Mexican Mafia.

That sounded kind of far-fetched, so I disregarded it. However, at what we will call "The End", at least of that story, these or other Mexican Mafia members came back and we never saw Ed again. Did he run away before they got there? Did they pull him, kicking and screaming, out of the house and kill him? Take him to Mexico? We never found out. I did recall one time he asked me repeatedly to take his name off my website, where it was for a short period of time. He must have known they were looking for him. A short time later, Al was contacted about some legal proceedings back in Illinois where this con man had been working before. He went back and testified. I don't think he saw Ed, so I don't know if he was being tried in absentia or what. I had a garage sale, then had Mexican women come and remove all clothing and personal belongings. Those women do a terrific job, that house was completely cleaned out."

"When was that, Dave?" dad asked.

"That was five years ago. My problem now is that a friend, a fellow vineyard lover of mine, has been holding up the vineyard since that time, covering costs, harvesting grapes and renting the house, but barely scraping by. Our agreement was 5 years, in which time I thought I'd have enough to buy back what has been his interest, but I don't have the money, so it will have to be sold, then all money will go to him, I won't get a dime, which is okay. I appreciate his holding up my dream for these five years. The vineyard is such a special place and I love it so much, I hate to lose it, but I've pretty much gotten used to the idea that it isn't mine any more. So sad, but there's nothing I can do. I can't reimburse him for the money he's owed. It would take one million to pull it out of hock and, even though there have been times in my career when I might have been able to scape that together, that time is past. It's okay, dad, I'm okay otherwise. You know it just breaks my heart, I loved that vineyard so much, just telling you about it is like losing it all over again. But, I love my wife and my kids are healthy, so I'm a wealthy man, even without a vineyard."

"That's the only way to look at it, Dave. I didn't plan on running a used car dealership, but you know, it's been okay. Now college kids get jobs at my lot and my mechanic is great, so it's a nice steady life. Maybe you can settle down some day soon. I wouldn't feel too bad about the vineyard. Something else might happen that cheers you up. Sorry you had to "re-live" it, but you'll go on and be okay. You know what they say,

"If you have your health, you have it all." and you do have that. I wish I could help you out."

Dad always had a way of settling things so everything was okay. He had survived, so he figured his kids would too.

"I do feel better having told you, dad. I knew all those years ago that some people cheat and you have to accept that that happens. As long as I'm breathing and have my family, I'll be fine."

"Speaking of breathing and family, Joslyn's only got three more laps! See you at dinner, Papa -- Italian!" Dave shouted over his shoulder as he trotted off toward the finish line to cheer in his little girl.

Mr Stohler looked forward to choking down that "eenie" food (linguine, zucchini, etc.) with his family. He really loved it, but he'd never admit it. It was better for him than French fries.

He'd sneak those later.

Joslyn's Points Race

"Come on, Joslyn, SPRINT!! SPRINT!!" Dave yelled. The race was getting closer to the finish now.

Joslyn could barely hear him, but his voice come through. She wasn't a sprinter, but she could put her head down and push her hardest time trial for the last two or three laps. She passed one girl... then another... she had lost track of who had how many points. She knew she had some, but wasn't sure how many others had right now. It sort of didn't matter because she was having a good race, and she could only do as well as she could do. She was having fun. Getting a place would be great, too!

Push, push!! Joslyn knew she was close to the leaders in points and there was only one more lap. Might she be able to get third? First and second were being contested in front of her between two girls who had about the same number of points, but whoever had the most points after them was a mystery. She passed the next girl. The familiar pain began, the pain that usually caused her to back off. But this was the Grand Prix! She HAD to keep it up, the girl she just passed DID have a sprint, so she'd have to stay ahead of her if she wanted to place -- if she had any chance. Keep ahead, keep ahead! Winning wasn't the issue, but she was having a good race and wanted to do her BEST!

Joslyn was struggling too, but she maintained her speed. They were on the back straight now with about 1/2 a lap left. The other girl who she thought had roughly the same points as herself pulled ahead.

Joslyn pushed harder. Could she? Could she? They were both gaining on the two girls in the lead, who were engaged in their own contest. They pulled within a 50 yards or so of the leaders. The finish line was coming up fast! Joslyn saw it and saw her dad waving her in. She put on one LAST burst of speed, but the girl next to her did the same, pulling ahead.

Joslyn kept up as hard a sprint as she was capable, even though it wasn't what you might call a "real" sprint. Getting out of the saddle was out of the question. Throwing the bike was a skill she had practiced, just for an occasion like this. She could feel another girl she had passed on the last lap coming up. Whoever crossed the finish line first would be third. Joslyn REALLY wanted that third, if that was possible. She had worked lap after lap to at least place in the top five, but third would be beyond her expectations.

Joslyn saw the other girl out of the corner of her eye. NO! She wasn't going to let her beat her! She could see how tired she was. Sprinters are known as "200 meter" riders, riders who can go REAL

FAST for 200 meters, but anything over that might be challenging. The other rider had started her sprint in turn two. The Baker Velodrome was 400 meters, so if a rider began their sprint in corner two, which is where many 200 meters begin on the more common 333 meter tracks, it was more than 200 meters from there to the finish line on the Baker velodrome. A Sprinter would be more likely to run out of steam! But a Pursuiter with a good sprint — like Joslyn — wouldn't. Joslyn put her head down and gave the last she had. As the finish line met her, Joslyn THREW her bike ahead, across the line, hoping,

hoping, hoping that she had won the third place medal. She heard it confirmed on the loudspeaker:

"Joslyn Stohler, third!" She knew how pleased the announcer was, he was another Little 500 winner, and he knew her dad. But oh, the pain... it was overwhelming. As she headed toward the warm-up track, Joslyn could hardly turn the pedals. She thought she might pass out, but that didn't happen. She couldn't wait to get off her bike just for a few minutes' recovery, then she'd warm down.

Joslyn saw her dad running exuberantly across the track toward her. He could hardly contain himself, grabbing her as soon as she got off her bike.

"Great race!" he shouted, picking her up in a bear hug of joy and swinging her around in the air. "I'm so proud of you!'

"Thanks, Dad!", she said gasped breathlessly as he put her down. And she promptly threw up on his expensive Italian shoes.

"Perfect!" he exclaimed happily, beaming proudly.

3. Cyril

Back when Dave got the job offer in Italy, Cyril applied to five colleges, and was accepted at four of them immediately. He decided on the University of Colorado. He liked the idea of the mountains and clean air. He also tried out for and made the college basketball team. He was a pretty good player (no matter what his dad said) and he did well. He was no star of the team, but the other guys could rely on him to pass the ball to the right guy to make the score. He didn't mind that the other guy got the glory, at least Cyril didn't have to feel bad he'd missed a basket, and he was happy just being an important part of the team. The other guys knew he had a gift of instant analysis for who was in the best position to score, more quickly than any of the others. He was seldom wrong, so the team was more likely to win when Cyril was playing.

Cyril had a couple of "friend" girlfriends, but once he got into his studies, he found he enjoyed college much more than he expected, and didn't have time for much of a social life. He didn't care, he felt busy and on a mission: graduate from college. There was a lot of freedom in college that he never experienced in high school. He could take whatever classes he wanted when he wanted to take them. He could even go a couple days a week and work a couple of days and put it all together into a busy, low key life. He was content.

He missed the gang, but he knew they were busy too, Dave off to Italy, Moocher and Nancy setting up their house and Mike -- well, there was no telling what Mike would do, but he didn't fit in Cyril's life as a friend separate from the group. He was always so cranky, if he hadn't known better, he would have thought Dave's dad was Mike's dad. Cranky... Mike was helping upgrade Moocher's house. That was nice of him, but Cyril also knew that it was partly because he didn't know what else to do with himself. It was better than getting into trouble. Mike had figured that much out, at least.

Cyril wasn't sure what he'd major in, but he thought he'd start with sociology ("Sosh"), after meeting a pretty girl who seemed to like him. But he had another objective too: "So I can figure people out. Especially my dad." When Mike heard his plan, he figured Cyril just wanted to meet girls, but he never did understand Cyril very well, in spite of all the time they'd spent together. Dave seemed to understand him with no explanation necessary, but Mike seemed to expect him to be someone other than who he was. Why do people do that? Cyril wanted to try and figure that out.

Once he started classes, Cyril found he was better prepared for school than he had expected. Studying came easy and he seemed to have a talent for class discussions that he had not realized before. People listened to him, just as though the thoughtful things he said bore some relevance to higher level thinking. He began feeling pretty good about his mind (no matter what his father said). He started thinking his father might be wrong. Dad, wrong!? That was a new idea to him. Cyril didn't need to accept low achievement. He began to feel he could really make a difference in the world.

The college had a counseling program, and Cyril went, just to find out what kinds of services they offered -- and because he had a paper due that he thought would be easier if the people at the counseling office told him things about the program, essentially writing the paper for him! It worked. *How College Counseling Centers Help Students Cope with College Pressures* got him an 'A'. As part of his inquiry, he realized that counseling might have something to offer him, so for the next year and a half, he went for weekly "chats" with a counselor who seemed to understand him -- or was at least willing to try. He worked through a lot of his uneasiness about his dad because he began to understand what a loving man he really was, even if he didn't know how to express it.

Eventually, the counselor suggested that Cyril take a psychology class to aid him in understanding his and other people's issues. The rest quickly became history: Cyril finally found his calling -- Psychology. It fit like a well-worn glove, and the world of people opened up to him. He read about many things that helped him understand his father that had never occurred to him, such as about the troubles of a man who was raised by a parent who had no understanding of children. Cyril began to realize that his dad was so "understanding" with him because he had felt so misunderstood by his own parents. Understanding his father released something within Cyril that drew him into studying psychology as a major, first at the Bachelor's degree level, then at Master's level, and finally for a PhD. Other people needed help understanding people too, so Cyril decided he'd like to teach.

Studying psychology didn't make Cyril feel smart as much as it stimulated his constant desire to know more about the wide variety of conditions within human hearts. He studied everything he could get his hands on, from the forefathers of modern psychological thought to some of the most challenging theories of child development and medications for all manner of psychological maladies. Why are we seeing so many children with autism? Why do some people have gender identification issues? What can we do about the soldiers returning from foreign wars with brain injuries and post traumatic stress syndromes? What possibilities do pharmacological solutions hold for these and other groups who need help? Are there alternatives that do not have horrible side effects? Cyril was not so much into drugs as he was finding solutions with the least negative impact to the person's physical structure. The brain fascinated him.

Cyril always kept up with the latest psychological theories, and loved diving into professional journals with his highest sensory projections toward possible solutions. His dream was to find The Big Answers, then write about them to help others. Cyril was a nice man, and brilliant in his published writings. While he had the excellent grasp of the scientific method expected by any well trained scientist, he also had a talent for ferreting out some new insight from within his data that others may not have seen, with each paper, large or small. Over time, other scientists studied his papers, not so much for the study results themselves, which they could readily see in the abstract, but for that "Cyril Thought", that suggestion, that twist on what, at first, seems obvious, but turns out to be unique. It had almost become a game to Cyril himself to attempt to "hide" the special little thought that spurred his colleagues into finding and accepting the challenge of the "proof inside the proof" that others might not see. Those who did, he saw as brilliant, not because they recognized his brilliance, but because they must have a gift for insight.

With this reputation, Cyril attracted the attention of one of the psychologists on the U. C. Denver campus via the inter-campus research site. Cyril was based in Colorado Springs, not so far away, but far enough that email and the net helped him communicate easier. He and the other psychologist began reading and enjoying each others' work. In "real life" she carried a level of glamor about her that deceived others into underestimating her competence, a source of chronic frustration for her, so she was much more comfortable communicating online so the other person wasn't distracted by the fact that she was female and beautiful. Her work was greatly appreciated until people met her and seemed distracted by her physical appearance, so she buried herself in research. She thoroughly enjoyed Cyril's work and its underlying humor. She read his papers and began corresponding with him online long before they actually met. They found that they saw many things similarly and had a lot in common so their online communications about studies and theories, both theirs and others, took on a life of its own. He read and offered insights to her work, and she did the same in return. With each paper he became more intrigued by her mind and some quirky ideas that seemed to pan out as more true than they initially appeared. "Wow", was all he was usually left with when reading her latest thoughts on some obscure line of inquiry.

Cyril initially mistook her interest in him as work-focused, when it was actually brain-focused. It was one brain matched with the other. It didn't occur to Cyril to do a net search to find out what she looked like, but Melody ran across a photograph of Cyril from the Little 500 with his name, among others, underneath. She figured out which one he was, the tall, gawky kid with intelligent eyes. She almost laughed when she realized one of those young boys in the plain t-shirt was her online genius.

"Ah, but by now, distinguished." she thought, doing a "computer aging" routine in her mind. There was the mass of curls surrounding an aquiline nose that she thought would look terribly professorial 30 years later. She could almost hear his voice delivering a lecture, even though she had never heard his voice. Truth was, she didn't care one whit about his physical appearance, she had found disappointment in "pretty boys" she had dated, and at least Cyril looked within the range of "normal". She knew that he was unlikely to be stuck on himself. She was more or less his "fan". There was only one problem she knew would raise it's ugly -- or in this case beautiful -- head. Would he be able to get by her stunning appearance or would he be stunned into silence like many colleagues she met? She was a beauty, with or without make-up, work clothes or ballgown. It too often disengaged communications from her surprised and distracted colleagues, quite a professional dilemma, which is why she never included photos in her communications with Cyril. She was so afraid her appearance would change that relationship of brain-to-brain that worked so well, so she didn't want to risk it.

Cyril found this unseen mind fascinating. They went into depth on many issues, offering each other ideas and suggestions for resources that they soon realized made both their work more profound and substantial. They really should work together, each thought. They could write grants and really dig in to making the world a better place. With this possibility in mind, Cyril finally proposed that they meet. If they could work together on joint studies offline (which would make a lot more sense) as well as they worked online, they'd make a great team!

The Date of Tea...

They set up the day and the place to meet to discuss all this further. He suggested they meet in a tea room downtown that he particularly liked. He thought he might impress his friend with his knowledge of tea. He knew a lot about varieties and their history, sort of as a hobby. Cyril was thrilled at the prospect of forming a symbiotic partnership with someone whose theories and ideas were so stimulating to his own.

He arrived at the tea house, accompanied by a paper he'd been working on. He wanted her opinion, so he arrived a little early. He wanted to read the paper through one last time before he gave it to her for her review. She told him that she had a paper for his review, too. Cyril sat the paper in front of him and settled down to wait. The tea room was fairly empty, plus, he had a good view of the door, so he could see when she arrived. It was only now that he wondered what she looked like, since he wanted to recognize her. He would find out soon. It was just about time for her to arrive. He wondered if she was the kind of woman who would arrive late, just to keep him waiting. She hadn't seemed like that. If she was on time, she should walk in the door now.

A man and woman left, holding the door for another couple, who looked like a duo from a Vogue magazine advertisement. Cyril thought "I guess the beautiful people have found this tea room, too."

The handsome man sat down at a table while the beautiful woman kept walking. Cyril knew the rest rooms weren't in his direction, so he assumed that she was simply choosing a different table and went back to his paper. Instead, she sat down next to him.

He wondered if she had some sort of question -- or maybe she recognized him from one of his lectures, though he was quite certain he would have remembered someone that stunning. He projected that she was meeting someone she didn't know and thought he was that person. Whatever she wanted, he would be polite, but he wished she didn't bother him while he waited for Melody, it might be awkward when she arrived. He looked up impatiently, waiting for the woman's question, which he would answer quickly and politely, so he could return to his paper. She was gorgeous, but he was had his mind on his research and was unmoved. He was waiting for The Woman with the Brilliant Mind.

"Dr Harrington?" she asked.

"Yes, can I help you? I'm just waiting for a friend." Cyril responded, with slight impatience.

"I'm Melody Anderson" she said, bluntly, then waited for his response.

He was stunned speechless. He had trouble reconciling the name.

"What?" He looked back at the entry door, expecting some scientific-looking person to enter at any moment. Then, all he could do was turn back to the Vogue model in disbelief.

"What?" He repeated. Could this be Melody?

Melody saw "The Look" as soon as he turned toward her. She sighed inwardly, then almost laughed. The poor guy. He looked so confused. She could appreciate that she had disturbed his concentration and she was flattered to realize how urgently he looked for a woman he could identify as "Melody" to walk in the door. She not only didn't look like the woman he'd imagined, he was completely unable to reconcile the reality of this beauty with "scientist".

She had described herself in an email: "I'm 5'8", around 135 lbs,

44

with dark, shoulder length hair", but this did not adequately describe the woman in front of him. Not hardly. Was this beauty really the brilliant scientist he'd been communicating with? Really? While he had enjoyed a low level flirtation in their communications, he took it as just friendly banter, nothing "real". He could not imagine this woman being interested in him, because he had seldom attracted beautiful women, not that looks were ever an issue to him. He prided himself on looking into the soul. He hoped she hadn't expected to meet someone who might make People Magazine's "Sexiest Man Alive". That wasn't him. He was a scientist, a "normal guy", he thought.

Melody was used to this silence, the temporary immobility of the man before her. She had endured men rendered speechless by her beauty all her life. She tried making herself look ugly by dressing down, wearing glasses and pulling her hair back, but none of that seemed to make any difference. Men still went silent and tried to whisper in her ear every time she went on a date. Finally, she just gave up on dating and dove into her work, which carried the added benefit of allowing her to show how brilliant she really was in a string of theoretical papers unrelated to looks. Once she began doing analytical studies, she came to Cyril's attention because she was one of the first to recognize his "little twist" talent for ferreting out what other researchers might overlook. Every time she found it and let him know, he thought she was brilliant.

"I recognized you from an old "Little 500" photo I found." She said.

"That was a long time ago." Cyril noted. They laughed. "Well then, you're the friend I was waiting for!" he said, relieved. They laughed again.

"Here, try some of this special blend of tea they just brought before you came in. It's my favorite. It's called 'Celebration.'" he said, as he poured her some of his favorite tea. She was glad the tension was broken. Maybe they could start communicating as fellow researchers now.

Within thirty seconds of her seeing "that look", Melody began pulling out her latest paper from her bag, almost as further proof she really was Melody. He relaxed when he saw that. It put his mind at ease. He looked forward to this from their discussions.

"Here's that analysis of Smith and Babcock's latest thesis you were looking at. I believe your response was spot on and here's my analysis of your response which as just been accepted by AERA *(American Educational Research Association)*. I'm not sure which publication it will appear in or if they'll ask me to present, but I thought you might like seeing it as part of our meeting."

Feeling warm and cozy from both his favorite tea and the visual pleasure of his new acquaintance, Cyril stuffed "stun" into the vaguest recesses of his brain and quickly moved into "researcher mode". Wow, he was relieved to have something to focus on aside from this beautiful creature in front of him. Thank heavens she brought something else for him to look at! He began reading her paper with the great interest, already peaked by her description, since he had been very interested in the work. God, she was beautiful! He decided that perhaps he'd been underestimating faces of Vogue models watching him from grocery aisles. Maybe they were smarter than he thought! He focused further on the paper.

With each word, each insight, "Melody the Vogue Model" was replaced by the "Melody the Brilliant Mind" person he had been communicating with, and he soon ceased to process the external view. The rest of their meeting was brain-to-brain. After the short transition, they managed to renew the partnership they had formerly only enjoyed online. It pretty much felt the same. From this time forward, though he knew it intellectually, Cyril never really saw her external beauty. He was in love with her mind.

Within a year of their meeting, Cyril and Melody had written 7 grants for themselves and their grad students and were married in the briefest of ceremonies. She became "Mel", transferring to the Colorado Springs branch of the University. Much to his surprise, Mel had ridden a bicycle for years, even competing at a lower level, just for the fun of it -- "just local stuff". When she let him know that she knew that he had been part of a champion bicycling team, no amount of protest at his minimal contribution could dissuade her certainty that they were made for each other.

Others could think he married her for her looks, but that was just their shallow thinking. She thought he was brilliant and he thought she was brilliant. Looks became anyone's issue but theirs, to her great relief. Cyril did periodically see "The Look" in the eyes of other men who met her. It quickly became a running joke, as they concentrated, brain to brain on their joint theories, and received good responses to their joint papers by people who had never seen Melody. Sometimes Cyril would meet with others without Melody specifically because neither one of them wanted to deal with "that". But, once discussion began, or the paper or research agreed upon, everything was always okay. Knowing Cyril really loved her, Melody found the "home" of being able to just be herself.

When Melody got pregnant, they celebrated with great joy. Cyril was terrified and overwhelmed with the idea of being a father. It was like entering foreign territory, but he participated in the birth and once little Marie was in his arms, every instinct of generations became clear to him. They named her Marie because they wanted a simple name that everyone would know and accept. Cyril was an odd name, and Cyril knew it. The name "Melody", along with her beauty, always seemed to add another underestimation, for her name as well as her looks -- which made her so mad it spurred her on to ever-higher achievement. They wanted Marie to have a clean slate. At first they were going to name her Mary, figuring that if she carried the name of Jesus' mother (even though neither of them were religious), how could they go wrong? The twist from the American "Mary" to the European "Marie" went along with their inability to ignore the little "twist" that they lived for, plus, for themselves, they had in mind naming her after scientist Marie Curie.

Cyril had great confidence in his little girl. Marie was so fiercely independent, it never bothered her that her grandfather always seemed to enjoy her failures -- plus, she didn't fail that often. Cyril wished he could have been that way when he was her age. She must have gotten that from her mother. If ever she got less than "A's" or lost a race, he just watched, amazed that she didn't seem to care about any setback she experienced. She just went at it again, as if it was just one more of life's challenges. She was used to her grandfather expressing his "great understanding" at failure, almost seeming to take pleasure in setbacks, but her dad made sure she didn't fall into that trap of feeling bad about it. He'd hated that. He expressed his pride in her, no matter what. She didn't really care what grandpa thought, anyway. She knew they both loved her. She almost felt sorry for Dad and Gramps, they took everything so seriously. Mel didn't take any of it personally either, that was their trip, not hers. She recognized it as left over from Cyril's childhood. To her, success or failure was a learning adventure for her. The same for Marie. After a while, Cyril's dad mellowed and began to laud achievements, much to

Cyril's surprise. He knew that Mel was largely responsible for this change in attitude -- she was such a brilliant psychologist, she had figured him out.

Cyril now seemed to see everyone and everything as a series of analyses, a by-product of his career. It was Mike who used to talk about Montana all the time, and even though Montana didn't intrigue him, the idea of beautiful mountains and wide open spaces -- with no tornadoes -- sounded great, so when Colorado accepted him for the permanent job in Colorado Springs, he was fine with it. Colorado hadn't disappointed him. Mel loved it there too, and it was a great town to bring up Marie. She rode her bike around town and got pulled into racing at the Olympic Velodrome — just for fun. It was so reminiscent of that great day in Bloomington, Cyril encouraged her and came up with the money for equipment - grumbling just a little, but then grandpa chipped in, too. He felt he had the best of all worlds. And now history had come full circle, because his little girl was going to be racing on the same track as his "brothers'" kids! Life was good.

Now they were all at the Jerry Baker velodrome, history smoothed out so they all looked forward to the trip and the races. Marie would be having fun at the upcoming races, as always.

Dave and Cyril

Dave watched a large man lumber toward him in the infield, accompanied by a young girl with wildly curly hair. He knew that walk, though he hadn't seen it for many years. It had to be Cyril, though he couldn't see him clearly yet because of the sun. The man went to the right of where Dave sat. As he passed, he could see the aquiline profile, and knew it was Cyril. Cyril hadn't seen him and was busy helping his girl spread out her blanket and set up chairs after carefully standing her bike up ready to ride. Cyril's daughter was tall, like him. She looked like a girl on a mission, paying little attention to her dad. He stood watching, waiting for her to need his help again. He didn't look completely comfortable, though the fact was, Cyril was never really comfortable unless presenting and lecturing.

Dave got up from his chair and stood for a moment, then started walking slowly toward Cyril. Cyril was oblivious until Dave was about 10 feet away then Cyril turned, wondering who was approaching his daughter. He looked at Dave without recognition at first, looking as though he expected an official or something, with all the cool cycling gear and cap, and he was ready to respond. All of a sudden a huge smile began inside and slowly spread up and over his face.

"Dave!" he exclaimed. "I hoped you'd be here! Come here -- how ya been?"

Cyril and Dave walked forward in a big warm hug only those with a shared history understand. They patted each others' backs. Truth was, Cyril was thrilled to see Dave, partly because he knew so little about track racing, even though they had one of the top facilities in the US in Colorado Springs. He had pretty much limited his involvement to viewing, and he was so busy with his work at the college, and he usually watched Marie's races while writing an article or correcting papers, so he didn't really know the rules, but that was okay, she was happy and that's all he cared about. He wasn't quite sure which race was up next or what was done. As many times as he referred to the race schedule, he never knew where they were in the program, it was somewhat of a mystery to him. He loved a good race, though. It inspired him to think Great Thoughts about Psychology and the next paper he was going to write related to human performance, while he watched his little girl love her ride and enjoy the "bicycle culture" he could plainly see she loved. If she won or lost, she didn't care, she just loved competing, sprints, endurance, she just rode. If she even placed in an event, she almost seemed embarrassed. That's his girl!

"And this is your little girl?" said Dave, with no doubt.

"Yes, this is my little baby Marie." replied Cyril, looking at her with great affection.

"Oh DAD!" exclaimed Marie, with no pause in her race preparations. She knew that was his way of saying "I love you", so she didn't really mind, but she wasn't sure who this older man was, so she made the token protest anyway. She figured that guy was probably one of the "brothers" dad talked about from time to time, but she'd have to meet him later. She still had to set up her rollers, set up her road bike for the warm-up and get going!

"Have you seen anyone else?" Cyril asked, knowing Dave would know what he meant.

Nancy had written all three of them that they and the others would be at the track this year. This was a REALLY exciting year, because it would be the first time they had seen each other in over 30 years. They looked around and, not spying either Mike or Moocher, they pulled their chairs up close together to catch up. It was just like yesterday... their relationship had not changed at all, no matter where they were.

4. Moocher

Growing up together, it seemed inevitable that Nancy and Moocher would finally tie the knot. Moocher figured it was inevitable, and besides, Nancy had always been one of the hard working, smart kids in school. And now, she worked! He didn't plan to let her be the only breadwinner for long, he'd find a way to pull his weight. It was a matter of principle.

Nancy's big job as Head Cashier came through fairly quickly after they got married, and she and Moocher began to plan a family. She didn't mind being the breadwinner, in fact, she liked it that way. Her home-life hadn't been the greatest, and working made her feel smart and competent. Moocher's dad stayed in Chicago, but the house didn't sell.

The old run-down house Moocher inherited from his parents. He and Nancy had initially tried to sell it, but they had no luck, so they realized they'd need to fix it up. It was no surprise no one wanted it, it was a mess. But Moocher and Nancy moved into it and started paying Moocher's dad some rent to help him out. Part of the deal was that they'd fix it up, and even buy it eventually, but they didn't have much money to do either in the beginning. Mike went over to help Moocher work on it. Moocher offered him a room, but Mike stayed with his brother because there was food on the table and he didn't have to cook it. Besides, he knew that Moocher didn't have a lot of money, and he didn't want to be a burden. He planned to just help them out when he could.

What neither of them expected was the children. Nancy got pregnant every few years until they decided five children were enough and Moocher got "clipped". It was easier than putting the burden on Nancy. Now the children were 29, 26, 19, 15 and 12. The last two were "unintended", but they didn't care, they loved all of their children unconditionally.

Fred was the first born. Moocher learned, at one time, that a "Fred" is a guy who's out riding a bicycle, but can't really ride very well. That's how he felt that day in Indy, in the 500. He was happy to help Dave out, but he had no idea what he was doing. That's why, after it was over and he was "a champion", he decided he'd learn everything he could about it.

Moocher named his first born Frederick partly because that race meant so much to him and partly because he thought it was a "name of substance", a name that belonged to scientists and stuff. The second one was named Beth, a tribute to Beth Heiden, who Moocher had watched in the '80 Olympics. They agreed that Nancy would pick the name of the third born. She named him Churchill.

"Churchill?" Moocher asked. "Churchill? You want to name him Churchill? What kind of name is that?"

"Yes," Nancy responded. "You've named Fred and Beth, I wanted a name that carried substantial weight in importance. We can come up with a nickname for him, if you don't want that for every day, but I want people to know that this child is substantial and important! I figure they'll recognize that name and won't forget it!"

Chilly was named after Winston Churchill. Nancy wanted to name him "Winston", but was afraid people might call him "Winny" and that wouldn't do. Nancy thought "Churchill" was a fine name for a boy to carry through life. "Churchill John", actually. Nancy gave him an "out" in case he hated the name. She never expected anyone to call him "Chilly", but that's what happened. And Chilly got teased, until he took up bike riding and won a few races. The nickname Chilly seemed a lot cooler then. Chilly was "the guy who won" a lot of the time. By the time Dave heard about it, Dave wasn't riding any more, but he felt the pride any uncle would feel in his progeny. The last two kids were also named after bike riders. Nelson, called "Nelly" was named after Nelson Vails. Finally the last one, after MUCH dispute, was named Connie, which Nancy advocated because as long as he was naming kids after cycling heroes, Connie was named after both a road champion (Connie Carpenter) and a track champion (Connie Paraskevin), so Moocher finally gave up on his first choice, "Rebecca" (after Rebecca Twigg).

The Big Mistake of Out-of-Towners...

Moocher was well known around Bloomington, which was both good and bad. He and his kids rode bicycles whenever possible. Every year, they ran into the same road hazard. Every year they suffered the same insults and underestimations from guys in cars all excited about the upcoming 500. They helped them learn the Joy of Bicycling.

Today, Moocher and Connie were riding, partly for business, partly for pleasure, as usual. Moocher rode in back, partly to protect Connie, partly because she liked riding in front.

He heard it first:

"Heeeeeeyyyyyyy bike-EEEEEE ! Hey little man... "

The Corvette came so close, Moocher thought he was going down. He heard the motor coming, but he then he figured it would just blow on by as usual. Not this time. He looked over at the newest jerks to come from out of town, thinking they were way too cool to have to give way to cyclists. Why did bikes take up all that room on the road? Anyone knows roads are for cars.

Moocher looked back at the road. They thought they could taunt him, even throw things at him -- you know, just to improve their aim and all -- just for fun. Hey, just some young dudes having fun. What could be wrong with that? He used to get really mad about it, but after all these years, he had finally learned to just shine it on and keep riding, putting in formal protests when they were REALLY out of line and otherwise just trying to adjust attitudes, one car/driver at a time.

But this buzz was different. This time, his 12-year-old, Connie, was riding in front of him, and the boys decided she was fair game too. Besides, she was a girl. They left Moocher and drove up next to Connie.

"Hey, little girl... You gonna come watch us in the 500? Look for us, because we're gonna win!" They pulled so close to her, Moocher accelerated to catch up. This was dangerous.

Moocher always watched the kids go nutty as the 500 drew close. Most kids in town, college kids and townies alike, knew about Moocher. Not only that he was a past 500 Champion, but that he had a little part time bike shop where college kids could come to learn about setting up their bikes and get hints on how to ride the race. Moocher didn't know much about bicycle riding or racing back when he was part of the winning team, but since he was the only one of the original Cutters team to stay in town, he became well known for that first victory and he worked real hard at rising to the level of knowledge that would warrant that additional respect. Especially when his kids got old enough, he wanted them to have a nice cheap way to get around town on their own, so he started hanging around the local bike shops to learn all he could, working, if they'd let him and not call him "Shorty". Now he knew as much about bicycle "stuff" as anyone in town, maybe even in the country, and so did his kids.

Each year, Moocher went to the 500 and helped with whatever was needed, from setting up chairs to truing wheels. He learned a lot about racing from that involvement, too, and now there were few people in town who understood what needed to happen to do well in the 500 (and not get knocked down) better than Moocher. Nancy had to put her foot down at one point, because there were so many college kids who tried to take advantage of Moocher's good nature and waste his time, asking him to build wheels, set up their bikes, get parts at cost -- she forced him to set part time hours and limit his work. His reputation built up over the years. If it was up to Moocher, the bike shop would never have made a dime, but, as usual, "Ms. Financial Manager" Nancy took the reins and they made a little money on the shop after all, plus saving money on bike purchases for the kids. Fred, Moocher's oldest boy, helped out too. Bicycling suited the family, everyone loved it. Plus, it gave them a special place in Bloomington.

But now Moocher's attention turned to his girl Connie, riding in front of him. The Corvette was driving close to her, too, and she was just a kid. She was a good bike handler, but she didn't deserve this treatment. Moocher watched, thinking they'd drive on, but they didn't. Connie kept her cool, but the Corvette jerks stayed close, yelling and generally trying to unnerve her. Moocher tried to allow his kids to fight their own battles, but Connie was still too young not to need a little protection. Moocher stood up, sprinting to the Corvette.

All of a sudden, he saw two cars and a bicycle surround the Corvette as Connie rode on steadily. One car stopped in front of the Corvette. The other stopped on the left side, blocking any sideways escape, as Moocher rode up in the rear. Moocher recognized the car that blocked the Corvette in front, a small sedan, driven by his son Nelly's former baby sitter Chrissy, now a college girl, who also rode a bike. When she saw them harassing Connie, she pulled in front and put on her brakes. They hadn't expected her to stop, and they almost rear-ended her. While hitting her would have been okay in theory -- just to teach her a lesson, you know, since it was her fault for stopping suddenly in front of them and all -- but they couldn't damage their precious Corvette, so they were really irritated at her move. They stopped to yell at her, while Connie rode on, slowly. A car approached on their left, pinning the "Vette" in. It was an SUV, driven by Connie's friend Scotty's dad. There was no escape for the Corvette. The guy who rode up on the bike had been out riding with two others, and coming the other way, when he saw the Corvette pass Moocher and approach Connie so he had sprinted ahead. His two riding companions had arrived by the time he approached the driver side window. Moocher had arrived by that time, too, but he watched the other rider, who he recognized from the University.

"You boys have a problem?" the bicyclist asked the boys in the Corvette.

"Hey, what are you doing?" came voices out of the car. "Get out of here, let us go! You can't block us in like this! We didn't mean anything, we were just playin' around!" The desperation in their voices contrasted with the arrogant tones a few minutes before. They hadn't expected to be held accountable for their behavior.

Connie stopped her bike and looked back, calmly watching the scene behind her, a replay of those she'd seen before. This wasn't the first time townspeople and college kids alike came to her aid. She knew the Corvette jerks were "just kidding" but she also knew they were dangerous. They were most dangerous because they were stupid, and showing off only made them more stupid. One of Connie's classmates ended up in the hospital because some jerky kid in a fancy car thought he could come to town and harass locals on bikes with no penalty. Throwing a milk bottle to knock her friend down had given them some jail time -- too bad it wasn't more than a few days. Her friend was in the hospital longer than that. Connie backed up to listen to what she knew would transpire. Her dad had gotten there by now, too.

"You know, we don't put up with harassment of bicyclists in this town. You new guys come here, thinking you're cool in your cool car and think nothing about harassing a girl minding her own business." said the bicyclist, who Moocher recognized as a professor at the University.

The Corvette jerks looked around for an escape, but they didn't see one, so they went silent, desperately trying to think of a way out. They tried not to look at the people surrounding them, but it wasn't easy.

"Aren't you in my history class? Tom Weber?" inquired the bicyclist.

The driver turned his face away trying to hide his embarrassment and humiliation. A few minutes ago, he was the Cool Dude in Town, answering to no one, and now he was not only trapped, this guy knew who he was. Great. Suddenly he didn't feel so cool. He was silent for a few minutes, then realized that he'd have to deal with what they'd done.

"Yes, sir, it's me. Hey, listen, we didn't mean anything by it, we were just joking around. I did something stupid. I'm embarrassed. This is my cousin Danny. He's just visiting and we were looking for something to do. I'm riding in the 500 next week, and I'm a little keyed up. I'm so embarrassed, I don't know what we were thinking."

"Okay, well, let me introduce you to whose kid you were harassing. This is the man everybody calls Moocher. He is the biggest giver to "all things Little 500" ever known. That was his girl you were harassing."

Tom looked, horrified, at the "little man" who had ridden up as they was being "captured". He didn't look like much. He had on jeans with a cuff clips and tennis shoes. Tom had seen him riding around town before, but didn't think anything of it. He didn't look like anyone spectacular or special. The kid had bike shorts and tennis shoes. They weren't racing, they were just out doing some chores. No need for an "outfit". But as unimpressed as Tom was with their outfits, he was stunned to realize that he had been harassing the legendary "Moocher", the Little 500 champion, small in stature, but huge in legend. He had planned to visit the "Little Bike Shop on Main" to learn some of the tips and hints he had heard were worth gold for anyone who seriously wanted to perform well in the 500, but hadn't managed to make it so far. Now his ship had sunk. The guy would never speak to him. A severe depression hit Tom. The others stared at him, not really enjoying his humiliation, but knowing that he was evaluating his own behavior. Every jerk needed a little time in front of witnesses.

"Oh my god, I am SO sorry, I had no idea!" Tom said in a small voice. Moocher had learned how to deal with these kids. He didn't excuse their behavior, but he had learned that he could usually turn the whole thing around and get a far better result than punching their lights out -- which he always felt like doing.

"Look, Tom -- Tom is it? You come on by my shop this Thursday and I'll fill you in on what you need to know about the 500. No grudge, no ill will. But from now on, if you see anyone doing what you were doing -- no matter WHO is doing that to WHOM -- I'd appreciate it if you'd defend the right of that person to ride without this kind of thing happening to them."

"I will! I am so embarrassed. Really, Mr Moocher, I promise I'll never do this kind of thing again." he said, disgusted with himself.

""Moocher" will do. Okay, I'll expect you Thursday. Bring your cousin if you want. If he's thinking of going to school here, we'd better indoctrinate him early". Moocher said, now with a twinkle in his eyes.

"Okay, and thank you." said Tom, thoroughly humiliated, but relieved. He couldn't wait to extricate himself from this situation.

"See you in class tomorrow. Paper due!" called the professor as he resumed his ride.

"Yes sir!" said Tom.

Tom came to the bike shop and Moocher shared his wisdom as generously as he did for any of the kids coming to him. He caught glimpses of Tom driving respectfully around bike riders from that time forward. One day he even saw him risk damage to his precious Corvette by blocking escape by some other young jerk who had been driving by a young college girl, harassing her on her way back to her dorm on her bike. Tom had gotten out and had a nice 'quiet' conversation with that kid, a kid who Moocher got to meet two days later. Tom had realized that if bicycling was safer for kids, it would benefit him too, so now he was a convert. Spreading the wisdom of bike culture takes time and patience, and Moocher had never been disappointed in his generous giving to this culture, as hard as it was to stay calm sometimes. It was this attitude and this ungrudging generosity that had won him the loyalty of the cross-culture of students and townies in Bloomington.

Moocher and Nancy

Moocher married a woman who loved him and accepted him just as he was, especially for his generous nature. Earlier in life, he had a knee jerk reaction of punching something whenever anyone referred to his height or weight, but, with Nancy's unconditional love and devotion, he had managed to learn to laugh at this former failing. He didn't need to prove anything to her or change anything about himself any more. This had enabled him to become more comfortable about everything as he found a new approach to living a happy life. He was now a contented man -- as long as people didn't threaten his kids or other bike riders — or call him "Shorty".

Nancy was a nice girl, who had set her sights on Moocher in third grade, when he got in a fight with another boy. The other boy, a boy who was quite a lot bigger than Moocher, had started the fight when he cut in line in front of the shy, quiet girl who Moocher liked. The girl started to cry to lose her place, but the big bully ignored her, looking like he was real proud of himself. Moocher knew what it was like to be bypassed and feel like you have no power, and he just wasn't going to stand watching this kind of thing. For some reason, Moocher had reached his tolerance with that behavior on that day, and protested that the boy should get in the back of the line.

When the bully asked "Do you want to make something of it?" Moocher replied "Yeah, I do!" as he stepped forward, knowing he might get hurt.

As the bigger boy approached and tried to grab him, Moocher managed to make contact just as the boy stumbled over a cement walkway barrier. When the boy felt the grab by Moocher, he didn't realize that what really happened is that he tripped and fell on his face. He was surprised that a little guy like this could punch him and make him fall down. He wasn't quite sure how it happened, but he was the one on the ground and his lip hurt. This little guy must have hit him! He had a new respect for this "little guy" and never challenged him again.

Seeing him hurt, Moocher knew what had happened, he hadn't hit him at all, but he felt it was justice, so he instantly came to the boy's aid, apologizing. He knew the other boy could have really hurt him if he'd connected. He helped the boy up. After he got back from the nurse (and in the back of the line), the other boy was nicer to Moocher. No apology, but that would have been too much to expect. Moocher was just as happy not to feel like he'd be pummeled for having the nerve to question the line cut. For some reason, the other boy now treated Moocher like they were friends, that day and ever since. Moocher learned his name was "Mike".

One thing Moocher figured out was that if you're a "little guy", it was a really good idea to make friends with the "big guys", like this guy Mike. He never expected them to be friends, because the other boy was rough, and not easy to talk to. But from that day on, they had a strange kind of friendship. Mike was tough and Moocher was kind. Mike needed kindness and Moocher needed a tough friend. And Nancy, who'd felt she had no power to kick this big bully out of the line, saw the whole thing, and stopped crying. Moocher was her hero from that day on.

Moocher originally bought his son Fred a bike because it was fun, plain and simple. Not only that, Fred started turning wrenches when he was three. Not really, of course, but he was trying. By now he was a REALLY good bike mechanic. As each of the other children grew big enough, they'd get a bike and Fred would teach them to ride.

The little part time bike shop was really more to save money

on buying bike parts for the kids, than because Moocher wanted to run a business, but he liked it. It came in handy because a bike was a lot cheaper than a car, and he and Nancy, in the early years, didn't have any extra money - or if they did, it was sent to help his dad. No one ever thought any of Moocher's kids would go to college, but Nancy had other ideas, and spent time after work helping the children with homework.

As the years went by, each child would help the next with school work, and so they grew up a close-knit family who all assumed they would help each other. Now Moocher and Nancy had five kids, and Nancy found time to work with each one, with Moocher's support. They had a very loving marriage, even though times were tough, especially with five kids, but they supported each other in all things and they gradually improved.

Moocher was a stay-at-home dad and found it suited him just fine. He didn't mind changing diapers or dealing with breast milk bottles Nancy pumped and left before leaving for work. In fact, he loved it, it made him feel needed. He loved kids and found a home life with Nancy that he never enjoyed with his own family. Nancy loved to work, but she loved her family too. She seemed to have endless energy. She spent 40 hours a week at her job and came home to a cooked meal that Moocher worked hard to make. Often it included vegetables he had picked from their garden. She brought home recipes, so they could create healthy meals for their kids together.

One day, when Nancy had the flu, they watched a TV show where some woman named Julia was showing how to do French cooking. It looked pretty easy, so Moocher started watching cooking shows more often between diaper changes and kids' naps. Soon he was experimenting with his own variations on the recipes and Nancy was bringing home fresh things from the store for him to cook. He had gotten pretty good at it, and was proud to have that skill to give to the family and support them with the best food available. He hadn't had such grand feasts when he was growing up, his dad had been lucky to have a can of Chef Boy-ar-dee to open and put on the table. Moocher didn't mind, he loved his dad and saw how hard things were for him, but he was also finding himself a talented chef, and that made the whole family happy.

Even when Nancy made Manager and they could afford it, they seldom went out because, by that time, the food just wasn't as good as they could make at home. Other people began noticing Moocher's talents and asked him to cater their birthday and other celebrations. Even though he didn't have too much time, it brought in a little extra money for clothes and new appliances -- and bicycle stuff. After he developed a reputation, he didn't have to advertise his bike shop and his fees went up, not because he was greedy, but because often he had to take time from other activities to do it. That was lucky, because college was expensive and he had five kids! They didn't all seem to want to go to college, but he and Nancy would be ready, just in case.

Things went well for Moocher's and Nancy's family. Moocher poured himself into the kids while Nancy moved up the ranks in business until she was a district manager, in charge of her own time and always looking for investments and ways to save money. It was like a game to her. She never underestimated the value of Moocher's role in supporting her and the children. She was able to do what she wanted to do because he pitched in and was always available to lend her support.

When one of the other managers "came on" to her at work one time, all she could do was laugh. As flattered as she was at the attention, she was unwavering in her life-mate choice of a man who wanted her to be all that she wanted to be, with no manly intimidation or ego. She knew who she was and what happiness was. As the kids grew up, she reveled in their activities. Now it appeared that her middle child, Chilly, was planning to compete in the Marymoor Grand Prix at the Jerry Baker Velodrome in Redmond, Washington, and she welcomed the trip as a family. Chilly had gone to the National Championships, aka "Nats", several times, but they had never gone to see him compete because the races were usually so far away and Moocher was so busy. But this year he had BIG plans. Race awards were big. Their familial Big Plans were to go cheer for Chilly's Greatest Moment. Win or lose didn't really matter to them, except that he'd be so happy if he won.

Moocher never liked the thought of leaving Bloomington. It was hard to think of traveling with all the kids plus equipment, even to go camping, but this Seattle area track race was different: it was a Grand Prix and "his boy" had a good chance to win one or two races. Moocher's COLLEGE boy. He hoped his old friends would be able to show up at the race. Nancy had written them all and BEGGED them to come. Fortunately, it didn't require too much persuasion.

Moocher had a lot to brag about, especially since he knew they didn't expect much of him in the old days, so, he loaded up the car and headed west. While some of it was boring driving, much of it was incredibly beautiful. Nancy had traveled a little with her parents while growing up and as part of her job, but Moocher had never been out of Indiana. He never saw any need. He loved his family and there was always something to do around the house. Now that he was on the road, he was glad for the new adventure. Life was opening up for him. He couldn't wait to see the racing. And, he was very excited about the prospect of seeing the other guys. He knew a little about what each was doing, thanks to Nancy, but not much in detail. He wondered how each of them had fared over the years. It sounded like they had all done well, Mike in the Marines -- they were so proud of him -- Cyril a college professor -- wow! -- and Dave, as they all expected, working for The Italians and traveling the world. Moocher didn't feel like his achievements matched theirs, but he knew he had had a successful life and that the others were proud of him too. He couldn't wait to see them again. He wondered if they had changed.

Mike and Marriage

Many things had happened to Mike since those early days of his new career. The Corps was good to him, in spite of some tough times mixed in. He'd decided to stay in as he traveled the world, learning a tremendous amount about life. He tried to keep in touch with the other "Cutters", but he quickly became busier than any of them. After 30 years of serving with pride, he was newly retired. The first thing he realized was how much "family time" he'd missed over those years.

He'd dreamed about this day the whole time. He had his self respect and had done as well as any of them. Truth was, he wasn't really sure exactly what all the others had done, but he knew he'd done right by the Corps and the Corps had done right by him. He had learned a lot about women, making the same mistakes many guys make. He knew from the start that he'd look GREAT in his uniform. By the time he signed up and got through Basic, he was a physical god. His work in the gym had become regular, partly because it just felt good. If ever he felt out of control, a good gym workout put him straight again.

He'd met a couple of women over the years who appreciated his great body, handsome face, and military bearing. He'd learned how to play the "Game of "Women". For some years, he played the field, and was the subject of more than one broken heart, but then he found Sissy, who was as "decked out" and in shape as he was. He decided she was The One, and asked her to marry him even though they hadn't known each other all that long. She was beautiful, smart, and she knew how to handle him. He was in love.

Unfortunately, she knew how to handle several other guys too, at the same time, and after about two years, Mike found out that although their marriage seemed great, in fact, it was great because she was so happy to have several men in her life. That was not acceptable. She attempted to reconcile, just the two of them at first, but then included a happy and enthusiastic suggestion of "group activities" that Mike found completely repulsive. From the moment she suggested such a thing, she was no longer his wife. The paperwork was just a detail. He got tested for any STD's immediately and that was the end of that. He was just happy he hadn't ended up with any diseases.

While the suddenness of it threw Mike for several months, every time he mentally recreated any scene including any of the men he knew about, he became nauseous and love was gone, with no regrets. He was surprised that he had no inkling of something being "different" about Sissy. She must have had incredible endurance. He knew one of the guys, Chuck, and although he liked Chuck, he was also now privy to his private life in a way that discontinued any further friendship that might have developed between them. Sissy married Chuck soon after the divorce, and the best Mike could do was wish them well, as he quashed imagery of their marriage that threatened to gag him.

The next episode of "The Women Game" went on for about a year. As much as he enjoyed all the adoration of women who appreciated his "machoness", Mike did miss the companionship of a regular woman in his life, but he was gun-shy of trying anything again very soon. One day, feeling especially lonely, he simply decided to just choose from among the women who were pursuing him. Instead of over-thinking a choice that might get him in trouble, he figured a nice, low-key, attractive -- but not too beautiful -- woman might be the ticket, so he settled on a nice, quiet gal named Elizabeth, a teller in his local back, who he had dated casually over several months. She always looked nice, very professional. They hadn't known each other very long, but Elizabeth seemed to need him. She always cheered up when he found her extra quiet, and that made him feel good. She didn't seem to chase guys, she had been married, and understood what a partnership meant. He often ran into her at Hurley's Tavern, near the bank where she worked. She just seemed like someone Mike could talk to. She eased his loneliness. She worked at a bank, she had a steady job. He proposed, and she said "Yes" on the spot.

"This one should work", he thought. "She's quiet and steady. And I like her. I need a nice companion. She's a bank teller, she should know how to handle money." Yes, this would work.

As soon as they were married, Elizabeth quit her job. Mike hadn't anticipated this. He thought she liked working at the bank, that it gave her a sense of purpose. She said she wanted to be a good wife, and that her greatest joy was fixing up the house and waiting for him to get home so they could have a nice relaxing glass of wine and talk about his day, before dinner. Everything was about him — he thought. Mike liked that. She wasn't out at the gym, picking up dudes, she was home, waiting for him, like a woman should be.

The surprise of this marriage occurred soon after they moved in together. After a few weeks of going home to a woman who hung on his every word, the day came when Mike got home about a half hour early. He wanted to surprise her, let her know how much he enjoyed their after work relaxation and her lovely dinners. She was a good cook. He had picked out a special bottle of wine. He called to her as he entered, and heard a panicked voice from the bathroom. At first, he thought she was hurt. She assured him that she was fine, she'd be right out. She sounded like she was putting something away. What was it? Maybe one of those "women things" that he never thought was any of his business.

Mike sat down to wait for their shared wine time. Elizabeth came out, straightening her shirt, and smoothing her hair. She offered no explanation and Mike didn't ask any more, but just sat with her, sharing their "wine time" and hoping everything was okay. She loved the wine he had picked out for this day. She seemed so relaxed and happy. They didn't discuss "whatever it was" further.

The next day was Elizabeth's shopping day. Mike knew she'd be gone for two hours in the afternoon. He decided to take a little side trip home and investigate, just to make sure everything was okay. He kept trying to tell himself everything was fine, but he'd been burned once for being too trusting and he felt uneasy.

When he entered the bathroom, he didn't notice anything out of place, but he felt that there must have been something she hadn't wanted him to see. He pulled out towels, looked in back of the medicine chest, looked in the cupboards, and found nothing. Maybe he was just imagining it.

He tried to recall the sounds he heard, what kinds of things were they? Hard surfaced things. After some searching, he took a good look at her cosmetics case. He quickly realized that it had a false bottom. When he opened it, he found a half-full bottle of bourbon. Bourbon? In her cosmetics case? What was that about? He recalled that she usually met him at the door with his glass of wine. He always liked that. But that also meant he wouldn't have noticed the smell of bourbon if she had been drinking. Was this a problem or just incidental? He recalled a few times when she had seemed unsteady, but he had chalked it up to her high heels. He never could figure out how women could walk in those things, but it was one of the things he found attractive about her, so he had dismissed it from his mind. He didn't realize there might have been another reason for her unsteadiness.

Mike went to the bank and had a confidential talk with the branch manager, who only spoke on condition of complete anonymity At first, he wouldn't talk to him, but then he recognized Mike from the Corps. They hadn't been in the same unit, but they recognized each other from around base. Mike begged for his help, which was hard for him to do, but he HAD to know.

"I could get fired if anyone found out I told you these things." the manager said.

"Don't worry," responded Mike. "They couldn't make me talk when I was a POW, there's no way I'd talk about this."

"Elizabeth was working at the bank as part of a community alcohol rehabilitation program. She did well, she was very conscientious and smart. But one time, not long before she quit, she returned from lunch smelling like alcohol. She seemed okay, but I know what it smells like. She was warned that she would be terminated if it ever happened again. I think there's a much longer history, but you'll have to ask Elizabeth about that."

Mike let out a big sigh, and went home to talk to Elizabeth, to see if there was any chance they might be able to salvage their relationship from what might be a very hard thing for her to deal with. It wasn't that he didn't understand alcoholism, he had lived with it during several segments of his life before and had realized how out of control and destructive it could be. He wanted to be fair and give Elizabeth a chance, even as much as he felt deceived.

"I think we need to talk", Mike said when he got back home. When Elizabeth met him at the door, she handed him his glass of wine.

"What, honey? Let's talk while we have our 'together time'". Elizabeth said, sweetly.

"I'll be right back." he said, and he walked to the bathroom. He grabbed her cosmetics case and brought it to the table, pushing it forward.

"I always thought this looked pretty big and heavy for a cosmetics case."

Elizabeth starred at the case, in silence. She took a gulp of her wine and looked back at the case. Tears started to fill her eyes.

"How did you find out?" she asked.

"Look, Elizabeth," he said as he leaned toward her and covered her hand with his. "I don't want this to be hard on either of us. I understand, I really do, but I can't have alcoholism in my life any more. I had it in my childhood, and it totally messed me up. Do you really love me or was I an escape? Do you think there's any hope for us, or are we living a lie?"

Elizabeth broke down. "Mike, you're much too nice a man to do this to. When you asked me to marry you, I was the happiest woman in the world, but it was more because I was about to get fired from the bank and was terrified. I really do like you, I know you're a good man, but if I'm truthful, I didn't marry you for love. I'm so sorry."

She confessed that she had been in rehab several times and had even tried suicide once. Mike was dumbfounded.

To Mike's credit, he didn't abandon the marriage. It was annulled on the grounds of "fraud", but Mike helped Elizabeth move to a group home where long term rehab care would be available until she could get back on her feet. She had severe emotional problems from an abusive childhood, in addition to the alcoholism, and although she was able to maintain a facade of health for a few weeks, both of them agreed that they got married for the wrong reasons.

Mike. He just didn't seem to be marriage material and he felt completely traumatized by the two times he had tried to settle down. Each time, he was so sure he had made a good choice. Each time, he thought he'd be happy.

But now Mike realized that he had made another big mistake and vowed never to get married again. Why did he have such trouble finding a nice, normal woman who was not either a nymphomaniac or an alcoholic? Was this too much to ask? She no longer needed to be beautiful or to revolve her life around his. She just needed to be honest, agreeable and genuinely like him -- to live life peacefully, day by day. Was this asking too much? Maybe he was just jinxed. Maybe he should just give up on expecting to have a nice woman in his life. Better to just play the "Game of Women" when he felt lonely and just focus on his career. He was due to be shipped out soon anyway.

Mike ended up at Camp Pendleton, near San Diego, where he met Julie. Julie was a physical therapist. He met her when he just came back from country and had a shoulder injury. She helped him SO much, including with some old injuries he suffered when he'd spent a month as a POW a few years before. She was older, older than him by a couple of years, but she was smart, not beautiful in the classic sense, but he just liked looking at her kindness, and she understood what he'd been through. She was in good physical shape, and was a hard worker. Mike respected that about her. When he looked at her he saw her giving to others, and that always made him feel good. They talked about his "wives" and life and travel and the Marine Corps. Mike told her all, not to gain her sympathy, but just so she'd know and understand that he was a little marriage shy. An emotionally stable woman with a purpose to her life that coincided with his interests seemed like just what he needed. It turned out, much to Mike's delight, that one of his old buddies from Basic had known Julie in high school and told Mike she was always a good person, active in sports and that she came from a good family. Good family was something Mike had looked for all his life. Maybe this one would work. Maybe it would work because he hadn't actually looked for it, it had just happened naturally, and felt comfortable and right. Julie had been married and was still on good terms with her ex-husband. That seemed like a good sign, too. She said their marriage had simply run its course, and, while she still loved him, it just seemed like the time came to go their separate ways, so they did, agreeably and with continued good will. That sounded a whole lot better than he had experienced and seen in other relationships.

Julie had gotten into physical therapy because she'd been a dancer, and went through some rough times trying to make it as a professional. She realized, at one point, that she just didn't have enough stamina, too many injuries from trying too hard, and she just lost the enthusiasm for exhaustion. However, she had always been fascinated with dance technique and how muscles performed in the various movements. At one point she got hurt, pulled a hamstring, and went for physical therapy. That was when dancing was her only aim. Once she got physical therapy and realized how much it could help other people, including other dancers, she became more and more fascinated with rehabilitation. After a few months in a training program, she decided this was her calling. She seemed to have a gift for it.

Julie and Mike settled down together, unmarried at first. They liked each other. She was a mature person with a career, so even though his assignments took him away for months at a time, she was busy and always happy to see him back. When he got reassigned, she went with him when she could, always finding work in physical therapy (PT) everywhere she went. "PT" was a good choice for a person who wanted to travel. Therapists were needed everywhere. They got married when Julie found out she was pregnant. When he was home, watching his little baby "Rosie" grow was his biggest joy. However, as she grew, it only seemed like he was gone for longer and longer stints. Sometimes he felt like he hardly knew his own wife and child, but no matter how much he traveled, his relationship with Julie was just the same when he got home. He really loved her for that. Eventually, they ended up back at Camp Pendleton. Rosie had been bitten by race fever, both on the road and on the track, but Mike had seldom been there to see her race. That was going to change.

Rosie

Rosie (Rosalia) found some old photos of dad winning the Little 500 and, picturing herself as "Daddy's Girl", she caught bike race fever. She had always had too much energy and she loved riding to calm down and get the world reset on its axis for her. There was good riding around Camp Pendleton. She could concentrate better and she felt great after each workout. Besides, she liked boys and LOVED to challenge them to sprints and show how great she was at climbing hills. San Diego had a track, and she went there for kids training programs, some by former Olympians. She rode with San Diego Bicycle Club sometimes, and tagged onto the "Wednesday rides" through Pendleton. As she grew up, she tried to learn everything she could about racing on the track, including learning how to do "co-ed" Madison races. One of her dreams was to win a co-ed Madison but that probably wouldn't happen for a while, though the great thing about San Diego was that they actually had co-ed Madisons.

Sometimes, Mike relived his singular day of track racing -- not adding too much detail to the story. Rosie didn't ask questions. Dad had been part of a Championship bicycle racing team on a track. She wanted that too.

Once she experienced success, she could think of nothing but racing. She lived it, breathed it, and imagined herself on the highest podium as she drifted off to sleep every night. She hadn't managed that high a step so far, especially at the national level. She'd done well in local races at the San Diego Velodrome, but big races like the Grand Prix brought out all the best riders in the US, and she'd never raced against many of them. She knew her dad would be there and wanted her to make him proud. That was her plan...

The Jerry Baker Velodrome was quite a bit bigger than San Diego's 333 meters that Rosie was used to. The Baker track was 400 meters, due to early years of allowing soccer in the infield. While the soccer had moved to another part of Marymoor Park, reconstructing a concrete track proved impossible, so it remained 400 meters. It wasn't really so bad, Rosie had watched old Goodwill Games videos of competition on Baker, and it looked like there was plenty of room for cameras, and for people to be able to see! In the films, people were seated completely all around the track. That wasn't possible in San Diego or many of the other tracks. She couldn't WAIT for competition. She'd been training for years, the last two on the track. Shaun Wallace, a British rider who adopted San Diego as his home track, helped her learn how to ride a track bike and had been teaching her a lot about Madison technique. It was one of his specialities and he had spent enough time in international competition to have a lot to teach. She adored him and followed ALL of his instructions. Olympic Coach Eddie Borysewicz had also taught her some techniques and helped her train when she could catch his workouts. He was tough, but she didn't mind. The tougher, the better, she figured. She tried to do everything her coaches told her to do.

The first thing Rosie had to learn was that a track bike was very different than the road bike she had learned to ride: it had NO BRAKES! and you couldn't stop pedaling unless you wanted to get thrown over the handlebars. At first, Rosie found it very intimidating, because of the "no brakes" thing and because she had to learn to ride on the slope of the track. She had watched other riders, so she knew that she wouldn't fall or slide down the track, but she still felt terrified the first time she tried to ride on the angle. But, as soon as she got used to the difference between a road and track bike, she happily exchanged one for the other and addiction set in even more. Track bikes felt great!

The road bike was heavier. She had to learn how to change the gears so that it was easier - or harder - depending on her choice, to pedal, especially up hills. She had to learn to keep pedaling during the shift, backing off on the pressure slightly so the gears would move smoothly into the new position. With practice, everything was easier.

Soon, she preferred the track bike to the road bike -- no shifting required! She just had to learn how to change the one gear on the bike with a wrench, according to where she was in the season and what event or workout she had planned. The bike was so light and elegant. It responded so directly to her pedaling. While it couldn't stop on a dime, it could slow quickly when she resisted the forward movement. It felt much more responsive and immediate. She loved the feel of it. She wanted another "fixie" to ride on the road, but dad wouldn't get it for her, he said it was too dangerous, even with a brake installed. She'd have to wait until she could get her own. As much as she enjoyed the group rides with San Diego Bike Club on her road bike, she soon came to love her track workouts best. They became like a drug, so focused and precise.

As she approached the sign-up table at Marymoor/Baker, Rosie saw a big group trying to register. Some guy in front of her didn't have enough money and was bartering with the guy doing registration. What was it with him? If he didn't have the money, he shouldn't be in line! Sigh... Well, that's okay, it gave her time to check out the guys -- and the other women she might be competing against. She could tell a lot by body type, but not necessarily. The sprinters tended to be thicker, while the distance guys and gals were usually thinner. She thought it was fun to project events for people according to body type, and then find out which events they actually rode.

"Hey, when did you get here?" she heard behind her.

She turned and saw her friend Maggie. Maggie trained in San Diego, same as her. They pretty much knew each other's strengths and weaknesses, but Rosie loved doing sprint and points races, while Maggie preferred endurance events, pursuits and other time trials on the track. Whenever they were in the same races, one of them did well, depending on whether it was a longer race or more of a sprinter's race. If one had a bad day and unexpectedly beat the other, it was fine, each was genuinely happy for the other.

"What all are you signing up for?" Rosie asked.

"Points, pursuit and scratch. What about you?"

"Sprints, of course, team sprint and the Madison. You are going to partner me in the Madison, aren't you? I don't have a partner yet."

"Sure! We'll be great! We've practiced enough, that's for sure!"

A few minutes later, Rosie listened carefully to a repeat of the loudspeaker announcement. She hadn't heard it clearly before, and she hoped it didn't say what she thought it said.

"The exhibition Madison has been changed to a co-ed event. If you've signed up with a partner of the same sex, you need to return to the registration area and re-register at the "Madison" table if you plan to participate in this event. Women, you must compete with a male. Men, you must have a woman as your partner." The announcer repeated the announcement for the third time. Rosie listened carefully and realized that she was not imagining it. It really DID say co-ed.

What??? She wanted to compete with Maggie! They planned to win! They were perfect partners, they knew each other. What was she going to do now? She didn't know any guys who would be available to partner with her. She would need a guy who had really GOOD endurance and who knows that she can go FAST for shorter periods of time. She wished some of the guys she rode with on the Wednesday rides were there to compete, but they raced the road events and not too many raced track. Another year, Brian might have raced track, but he just got a new job, so he skipped this year. He had to save for college and didn't think he could win enough racing his bike.

Rosie walked over to the registration table. She walked up to the table as tears of frustration filled her eyes. Damn! She didn't want to do this, it's SO "weak female"! -- but she was so desperate to ride the Madison and it wasn't fair that she couldn't! She was getting really GOOD at it! The tears came for a few minutes, then she straightened up. It was lucky not many people were around, since there was a race going on. Some guy came from out of the back of the tent and offered her a Kleenex. She took it, embarrassed, but not much else mattered except her race, so the tears were just details. She HAD to find a partner!

"Okay, do you feel better now?" the guy behind the registration table was kind and sympathetic. He'd better not think she was soft. She wasn't! She was her father's daughter, she was MAD.

"I'm not really upset, I'm just so mad! I had this planned out with my friend. We've been getting some really great coaching and we're really GOOD, and we planned to win it! Now I have no partner and neither does she!"

"I'm really sorry, do you understand why it got changed?"

"No, I don't! We registered as partners and now we have no race!"

"Well, the reason it got changed is because a big prize has been added. I mean a BIG prize. Prizes for the top three - maybe even five. The couple putting up the prizes said that since this is an exhibition race and not a National Championship, they wanted it to be more fun for the crowd and they also wanted it to be BIG for the riders. They used to race, and they never got much money for it. They couldn't compete in team races in their day, as much fun as they thought that might be. Plus, they wanted to make a bigger contribution to riders who were willing to do a race that is more fun and unexpected. They said they admire riders who are willing to try new things. When they were racing, things weren't so predictable. Plus, they raced in Europe, and they used to get prizes like a couch and three pheasants and all sorts of unexpected things. They thought it made it more fun. Now, they wanted to make a contribution and make it fun. Part of the deal is that they wanted it to be co-ed, just like the race they might have loved to do if it were possible in their day."

Hmmm now this made it more interesting, for sure. Rosie stepped aside to think about it a little. She'd have to adjust to this big change. Maggie DID say she was feeling pretty tired from her races.

"What are the prizes?"

The guy who had handed her the Kleenex spoke up.

"First is $5,000, second is $3,500, third is $2,000. They might add two more places, but they want to see the racing first. That will strictly be a surprise."

Holy moly! That would be worth riding with anyone who could maintain speed over distance! Where could she find a partner last minute like this? Just then, another woman walked up to the table.

"Chilly!" she called to the guy in the back. He came out.

"Hi! Are you ready?" He asked, cheerily.

"Look, I hate to tell you this, but I don't think I can ride."

"What? No, don't tell me that, we can win this thing! Come on, Ashley, you can do it, you're tough!"

"I'm so sorry, Chilly, but I just can't. I'm dropping out of Keirin, too. I'm just way too tired, I've been racing too much lately."

"Ashley, please, don't let me down. Did you hear the prizes?"

"Yes, I'm so sorry, if I could possibly do it, I would. I'd only let you down, and you deserve better. I need to tell you now so you have time to find another partner."

Chilly looked at her, crest-fallen. He had counted on her to help HIM win the race. He was in great shape and even though Ashley was better at shorter distances, that didn't matter, he had great speed endurance, especially on the track. He could compensate for her fatigue. On the other hand, $5,000 was enough to make for some pretty desperate competition, and Chilly also didn't want to come in sixth. That would only break his heart.

He looked at Rosie in tears and suddenly fully understood her predicament. Both of them had gotten the rug pulled out from under them. He wasn't going to cry, though he felt like it, but he was sure going to do a sprint to look for someone who could help him win. There was more than winning a race at this point, for him. He planned to beat Andy Mathews, a totally self-absorbed rider who was the bane of Chilly's existence. It wasn't that Andy beat Chilly, it was his sense of entitlement that he was the best, and that this little scrawny guy from Bloomington couldn't compete with him. It really peeved Chilly. Sure, Andy had beaten him a few times, but they were actually pretty even for number of races and who won and usually there was some team blocking or something that made it not a clean competition.

Chilly knew Andy was a decent rider, and was willing to give Andy the appropriate respect, but Andy never reciprocated. He always had some phony excuse for why he lost, and his team seemed to accept his excuses as truth instead of the truth being that Chilly had beaten him that day. He thought of Andy and his team as the Indy Mafia. They had ready access to the Indy track, and spent more time on it than Chilly, since his home was 60 miles away. They had "home track advantage". Well, this time the track was neutral, plus, the longer the track, the better it suited Chilly. He had great endurance, and always had. The longer flat sections should be better for him. Now if he could just find a girl with a sprint who also had some endurance. The Madison would be 80 laps over 400 meters. 20 miles. A long race for the track. It would be nice if he could find a girl who could handle both the distance and the speed.

"How about you, do you have a partner?" Rosie asked, desperately.

"No, but I have someone in mind." Chilly said, lying because he had never seen this girl before. She looked fit enough, but that doesn't always mean anything. Could she ride? Did she know how to do Madison exchanges? Grabbing a partner at speed and throwing them into the race took a LOT of practice and some natural talent, at least at the level Chilly planned. The last thing he wanted to do was get knocked down because some girl didn't know how to do the exchanges or how to grab and throw. No, he needed someone he knew had experience, like Ashley. The trouble was, she was the only girl he knew who could do a decent Madison in Indy. There were others who were learning or could do it, but not at a competitive level -- not at Chilly's level. Competition is completely different.

Chilly returned to the infield. He saw his friend Bill and walked to him quickly.

"Hey! I need a partner for the Madison, do you know any fast women who have some endurance?"

"Sure, Sheryl, but she's already on a team."

"Oh thanks," said Chilly, "Big help."

"Well, let me see... the trouble is, they have to be able to throw, or at least touch hands without getting in the way or knocking anyone down. Riding's one thing, Madison's another. Let's see... Hey! How about Kisha? She's fast and gutsy."

"I need fast and upright. Leave "gutsy" for another day. If I can just find the right partner, I know I can win this thing." said Chilly. Chilly walked on, looking for Kisha.

"Kisha!" Chilly called, approaching the warm up track. Kisha slowed, coming to a stop in front of Chilly.

"What?" Kisha asked. "Do you need some tools? They're in my tent, ask Sam to help you, use anything you want."

She didn't know Chilly well, but they had been at several events together, and she knew he was a good guy, she could trust him. She usually rode in T-Town (also known as Trexlertown) near Allentown, Pennsylvania. They had a great training program and taught Kisha how to do Madison throws and how to ride in a pack.

"No, I need a Madison partner. Are you on a team? Do you have a partner yet? You do know how to ride Madisons, don't you?"

"Oh wow, well, I know how to do it and I've done a few Madisons with some success, but I got knocked down a couple of weeks ago and I've kind of lost my nerve for now. It's getting better, but I'm still very skittish and I know how you ride, Chilly, I could never keep up with you. I could sure use the money, but I really can't do it today. Keep me in mind for next year!" Kisha said, with regret.

"Dang," said Chilly. "I understand, I really do, but are you SURE you can't do it? I thought I saw you ride a Madison last time I was in T-Town and you looked pretty good!"

"Yeah, well, I was improving, and I love Madisons, I'm just spooked right now. I don't want to be the person that causes you to get last or get knocked down. Really, Chilly, I'd love to, but I just can't. Catch me next year, I'd love to partner!"

Chilly accepted it, disheartened though it made him feel. The high pace of a Madison really would be scary and cause a lot of trouble for someone with a confidence problem. He looked around the track, hoping to see someone who might be a suitable partner.

A sprint event was starting soon. He guessed he'd settle down and watch it. The Madison wasn't until tomorrow, maybe he'd find a partner by then. He'd put the word out. Meanwhile, he'd check out the girl who had been crying at registration. She looked like she was up in this event. It was just a sprint, so he'd know quickly if she had any "chops" — and guts and speed.

Rosie's Sprint

Rosie had been sitting, in all her gear, waiting by the start line. She no longer thought about the Madison. She was going to be competing in the Sprint, a strategic game of "cat and mouse".

This would be a tough race. Her competition sat to her left a rider named Joan. The ref went over, offering the drawing of lots in a bag to determine who would be up track or down. That done, it would be time to start. She wanted to do well. She reached into the bag and pulled out a lot that indicated she would lead the first lap.

Rosie had a bad case of nerves in this one. She'd ridden hundreds of sprints, but this one was different. This one had her dad in the stands, watching her every move. She knew he loved her more than life, but she also knew that he would expect the same degree of discipline he knew from a military life. She wasn't military, she was still a kid. She wasn't ready to fulfill someone else's idea of supreme discipline she knew he expected. And, if she was truthful, she didn't think she could live up to his expectations anyway.

She hadn't spent a lot of time with him in probably about 10 years. He took her to see a bike race at a track in Germany a long time ago, and it was SO exciting! The stands were completely full and everyone was screaming with the thrill of the race! She didn't imagine herself riding on a track until she moved to San Diego. That seemed so long ago. She competed in the last five National Championships, and she was always improving. But at the Grand Prix she was riding for the WIN! She thought she had a good chance. But she'd thought that before, only to be disappointed with second, or even third. Once she got skunked early and didn't even make it to the final rounds. That would never happen again. She knew a lot more about how to get to the Finals now. It takes strategy, strategy she had learned from Shaun Wallace, Eddie B., and other riders.

The first time Rosie made it to the podium in Nationals, it was for fifth, the lowest of the places on the podium and receiving awards.

She thought that was her best dream at the time, because she hadn't made it to podiums at all except for children's races, when they give out many medals and ribbons just to encourage kids to race. But once she got to fifth, that medal only made her believe that she could climb higher -- literally and figuratively. And she did. But she still hadn't made it to the top, #1, the National Champion. She thought she'd be happy if she achieved that, but a small part inside of her knew that the truth was, she really just wanted to know how far she could go. She was only 19, so it wasn't like she didn't have some time left, but this year was different. Every year was different.

Rosie heard the announcement for riders in the Sprint to line up (there were only two, her and Joan) at the start. She'd been nervous ever since the previous race had started, knowing hers was next. She gathered up her stuff and tried to relax until it was time to mount her bike. She was warmed up and ready. She'd gotten this bike last year. She didn't want a new one because this one rode great, and she was used to it. Shoes fit great, gloves and shorts were comfortable. She'd gotten a new helmet, of course, but that's because, to some degree, it was a fashion statement. The bike could be last year's, but the helmet needed to be COOL. Hers was. When dad asked her what she wanted for her birthday, her answer was this helmet. This $300 helmet. Dad was happy to get it for her. He would have bought her a new bike if she'd asked for it. Money was nothing compared to his love for Rosie. She had been the soft, lovely, little precious one whose photo had spent so many nights with him when he was on duty. The month he'd spent as a POW, his captors left it with him, trying to torment him with telling him over and over that he'd never see her again. It had the opposite effect -- she became what he lived for. When they did the prisoner exchange, he held it out to one of his guards and said "I'm going home to her now!" The guard just stared back at him. If ever he wondered who he was there for, he'd just take out his wallet and he'd know right away.

Rosie readied herself at the start line of the sprint in the lower (lead) position on the track. You would think that a sprint race would be like the track and field sprint races you see on TV, where the gun goes off and everyone runs as fast as they can — in this case, peddling as fast as they can. But not in this race on the track. In this race, 2 riders spend the 1st lap watching each other, cat and mouse, wondering what kind of a race the other rider has planned. If two riders have raced together before, they probably have a pretty good idea of what kind of a race the other rider will expect. So part of your strategy is to surprise the person who thinks they know you. If the other rider is new to you, and you are a rider who has raced for the last few years, the new person is probably not very experienced or maybe a transplant from some other situation. The person you worry about is someone that you know has been good year after year. Chances are they'll be good this year, too. The question becomes: "Are you better?" Rosie was about to find out.

Rosie put her bike next to Joan's without looking at her. She hoped to unleash some sort of surprise, but wasn't quite sure what that might be. Her own surprise would be to figure out a surprise!

The biggest surprise she could think of for Joan was for her to think Rosie might beat her or even give her a good contest. To Joan, Rosie was an "also ran", a rider she could always beat. Well, that may have been true in the past, but Rosie had learned a lot from her workouts with Shaun Wallace and Eddie "B"', and she had recently beaten some guys she thought were pretty good. She was feeling more confident than Joan might expect, but she decided being underestimated was good.

Joan had won the Sprint championship for the last 2 years. She was very experienced and had great coaching and parent support. She was gutsy, and she easily intimidated Rosie. While Rosie knew that getting knocked down was a possibility, she was a pretty good bike handler, and could usually take care of herself, but she also knew that her best strategy was to stay away from Joan and not run the risk that they would get into physical contact. This was not always easy. Although sprinters are not supposed to make contact during the race, it is something that often happens in the heat of the moment.

"We need a holder here!" Rosie heard one of the officials shout, to no one in particular. It made her uneasy to have some unknown person hold her, but the San Diego track folks were busy. There were things to know when acting as "holder". How to help her find her best start position without her falling over. How to push her off so that she moved forward strongly, but steadily. Her fear was that some guy would push her to a wobbly, bad start.

She saw a guy spring up from a nearby chair and run over. Rosie's "holder", the guy holding her up at the beginning of the race, was some guy who said his name was "Dave". He seemed to know how to do it. He asked her which foot she preferred forward, held her securely, lifting her on the bike so she could find her "spot", and immediately followed every request she made of him. He did not waver, he was strong and practiced. She didn't know who he was, but he seemed to know what he was doing and that was a relief. She could relax. No doubt he'd push her off right.

Rosie clicked her shoes into the pedals and pulled the straps tight. This race would not be long enough for any kind of pressure or pain in her feet to be an issue. The threat of "pulling a foot" from the pedal was much more threatening. That could lose the race right there in some situations, if not cause a crash. She adjusted and readjusted her position. She put her hands on her helmet, adjusting it, at her leisure.

Rosie had already learned about starting line intimidation. Some riders "needed" to put off dropping to the bars until the other rider had gone to the bars first. It was some sort of power thing Rosie didn't have much patience for. "Come on, let's light this candle!" was what she usually thought, but she was also aware that she could take all the time she wanted to get ready, to get set, and then to GO at the referee's whistle. There was no gun to signal the start of this race because it followed certain rules, depending on how the riders involved chose to ride it. This race often boiled down to the last 200 meters. Once The Sprint started, within the race itself, it became "no holds barred", all out, first-one-to-the-line battle.

Right before she went down on the bars, Rosie focused and held her position, getting her breathing under control. This guy Dave whispered a few things in her ear so that Joan could not hear.

"Baker is a longer track. If you have a long sprint, start it sooner, because your 300 meters might make it to the finish ahead of her 200. Just relax and have fun."

He was right. But how did he know? She hadn't been quite sure what she'd do, exactly, but he was right, this was a longer track. It might "throw" Joan to try the same kind of sprint she usually did on this 400 meter track as she would on a 250 or 333 meter track, the more common distance. Joan was used to a 250 track. Rosie did have a longer sprint, which had allowed her to beat more than one competitor in the past. But those sprint distances were usually contested over three laps on the shorter track, while Baker sprint distance only went for two laps. Aside from Joan not being used to this track, the longer track plus less laps might throw her off just enough... Rosie kept those factors in mind.

Some sprinters can hold speed for longer than the traditional final 200 meters. One guy she heard about was well known for being able to continually accelerate, no matter how long the distance of the sprint. Rosie wanted to do that, too. Some "sprinters" don't have as fast a top end, but can hold a high level of speed over a longer distance than most other sprinters. Others had a "blast", but petered out quickly. Sometimes sprinters would try the strategy of surprising the other competitor by starting the sprint much too early for a traditional sprint and try to "kilo" the competition over the whole distance, riding as hard as they can from the beginning. That was a REAL gamble! But, if they could get enough of a lead in their surprise and if they had what might be thought of as a "long sprint", sometimes this strategy was successful. It was all like some sort of miserable math word problem:

"If Rider X can hold ___ (high) speed over 200 meters, how far ahead of Rider X does Rider Y have to be and at ___ (lower, but still fast) speed, in order to beat him/her in a sprint?"

The only trouble with this formula would be the corollary:

"If either rider has a ride of better or less speed on that day, then what happens?" It would be a wild card.

Rosie knew that part of the challenge of sprint is what she and the other rider chooses to do in any part of the sprint. And you never really know what that is until the race starts. Looking for that "sweet spot" of a tiny moment of lost concentration by the other rider, that moment when they're looking for you on their left and you JUMP on their right... Finding those moments and reacting instantly within them increased chances of winning. Riders try very hard to mix it up to assure surprise. If they're too predicable, that's no good. What Rosie knew is that Joan wouldn't expect a real challenge.

Rosie decided she was ready. She dropped down on the bars, nodding at the ref. She already knew that Joan would not drop to the bars until she did. So what? That has nothing to do with the race, and if Joan thought Rosie was intimidated by some sort of war of nerves as to who would drop to the bars first, she was mistaken. Rosie had gotten over that long ago. It was the search for the "sweet spot" of surprise that plagued Rosie when competing with another top rider, none of that stupid "bar competition". She could only roll her eyes at that.

The ref looked at Joan, who had finally gotten down on the bars. She shook her head "ready". The ref blew softly and briefly into the whistle. Dave gave Rosie a strong, forward push. It starts...

The Cat and the Mouse

Rosie didn't really expect to win this race, but she was not going to make it easy for Joan, either. She would have to lead the first lap, according to the rules. Okay, fine. She didn't think Joan would try to "kilo" her (try to take off from the start and sprint for two laps), because Joan knew Rosie had good endurance -- probably better than Joan. Joan's gift was in her blazing speed over the 200 meter distance. They'd just have to play it out and see.

As Rosie peddled steadily around on the first lap, she dipped a time or two, just to test Joan's responses. Joan only took a millisecond to respond. Tricking her would not be easy. Rosie went down on the backstretch, peddling steadily, then back up the turn three banking. Joan stayed on her wheel all the way, finding her slipstream again with each move Rosie attempted.

One of the things Rosie knew about Joan is that she was a "from the back" rider. She didn't like being on the front and having to constantly look over her shoulder. Rosie, on the other hand, didn't mind whether she started in back or in front, but she preferred being in the back a teeny bit, plus, she'd rather put Joan where she was least comfortable, so she decided to force Joan to the front. If Joan was going to pull this prima donna stuff of having to be the last down on the drops, she could just be forced to the front. Everything couldn't be her way. Rosie always felt like she was like her dad when she got this obstinate, "they can't do that to me!" urge.

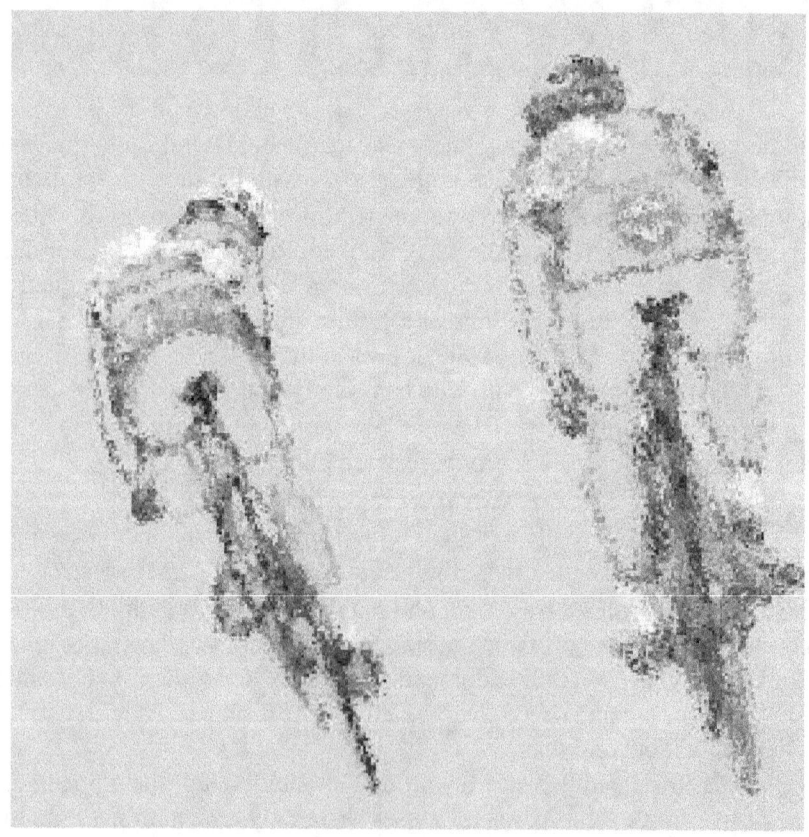

She couldn't force Joan to take the front until the end of the first lap - it was the rules. Until then, they had to maintain at least a "walking pace" and refs would often walk along with them to assure that pace. As they reached the starting line, Rosie slowed. Joan knew what she had in mind, and was happy to rise to the challenge: a track stand.

"No no, little girl." Joan said inside herself, "you're NOT going to force me to the front!"

"Oh yes I am!" Rosie replied, also within herself. Each knew what the other was thinking. While both were good at this skill, one would usually give in, either from impatience or just not feeling quite as "fine tuned" that day. Neither wanted to fall over, especially in front of a crowd. Either could have an "off-day". Rosie was hoping that today it would be Joan, because she felt terrific, as though she could stay "sur place" (as the French called it) all day.

Rosie planted herself, right foot front, balancing on her bike. She hopped her bike until she felt it was in a comfortable position. It had taken a lot of practice to get good at a track stand, but she was really good at it now. Joan rode close, trying to intimidate her and break her concentration. She also stopped, adjusted her position, and stood still,

 moving her pedals forth and back in order to maintain her balance and hope to throw Rosie's concentration off. They stopped, while the crowd watched breathlessly, waiting to see which woman would falter and have to take the lead. Rosie knew that crowds loved track stands, wondering who would have to move forward first, for whatever reason, either by choice or because they couldn't stop and not fall over.

Another of Rosie's gifts from her dad, besides obstinateness, was coordination. She could stand on her bike until the cows came home, with little shakiness. Sometimes she did it in pubic just to surprise people -- a "girl" who could do "sur place". It did require some natural talent, and that happened to be one of Rosie's. She was SURE she could hold it longer than Joan today. She waited, looking down, trying to stay relaxed even as she held the position. For some reason she couldn't explain, she felt Joan falter. It wasn't something anyone else could see, it was more like her energy field became lessened as she stood. Joan crept forward slowly, moving around Rosie and up track. Rosie, showing no reaction, followed her.

"Good move, Rosie!" she could hear Dave's voice.

On most tracks, the 200 meter sprint line begins in the descent area in turn 2, and riders can quickly build up speed when accelerating on the descent. The last 200 meters, on the Baker Velodrome, begins part way into the flat backstretch on the last lap, so to take advantage of the acceleration on the descent, the sprint would be more like 300 meters. Rosie had decided, after Dave had whispered in her ear, that her best move was to 1) catch Joan by surprise and 2) take a flyer down the banking just BEFORE turn two in order to build speed, which she would then maintain in her longer sprint. The distance was so long, she figured Joan wouldn't expect that. Now if she could just find that sweet spot...

No matter what Rosie decided to do, it would be tricky to trick an experienced sprinter like Joan. Both riders advanced on the turn 1 - turn 2 banking. They were headed for turn 2, where Rosie anticipated that Joan would make her move. It didn't make any sense to try to pick up speed on a flat backstretch, she'd want to dive down on the turn 2 banking. So, how could Rosie surprise her in a situation so predictable?

Rosie began to "play" with Joan. Joan, unalarmed, recognized it. She had to keep looking behind her, which is why she didn't like the front. A smart rider could take advantage of some small moment and turn it into a win. Joan did expect that Rosie might try to take a flyer, so she was watching for it. What she didn't expect was what Rosie did.

Rosie dipped down, causing Joan to look left. Then she pulled up track, over the top of where Joan was, causing her to look right. Then she backed off momentarily, causing Joan to look forward, planning her descent into her sprint, that she knew was coming soon. But before she realized it, Rosie let fly with her sprint, from the top of the banking, crossing in front of Joan -- but not obstructing her course -- down track, gaining speed over the whole way. It wasn't so much that Joan couldn't keep up with her, she just didn't expect Rosie to do what she did and she couldn't believe it for a moment.

That's NOT what sprinters do. They don't try to go over the top because it's too easy for the person down track to jump on their wheel, enjoying wind protection all the way to the finish line. But Rosie did it so quickly and unexpectedly, so well timed, that Joan was still looking left a little down track when she felt the wind of Rosie's jump -- for an instant.

Then she reacted, but way later then she would have preferred, plus, she was about a third of the way down track, so she couldn't take full advantage of the banking to accelerate, like Rosie had done.

Joan's adrenaline spiked as she accelerated down the banking after Rosie, who was now on the flat backstretch as Joan was still accelerating. She thought she'd have no trouble catching Rosie, and began closing the distance immediately, but felt the long backstretch go ON and ON, taking its toll on her sprint. Finally, she reached turn 3, seeing Rosie solidly in the sprint lane in front of her. Joan was gaining, but she knew that this sprint would be way more than 200 meters, her forte. Rosie "felt" her coming up, partly because she could see her out of the corner of her eye, but mostly because of the steadily increasing roar of the crowd. Then she realized that Joan had reached her back wheel and it's wind protection. Next would come Joan's attempt to come around her, continuing to accelerate to the finish line. That would be the classic move -- on a 250 or 333 track.

When Joan was trying to come around, Rosie poured on her sprint, maintaining her speed along side this more experienced sprinter with everything she had.

The crowd was cheering wildly, not really caring which one would win as much as they loved a great race, and this certainly turned out to be more than they expected. Rosie saw her holder Dave in the turn 4 infield, who had his cap off and was energetically throwing Rosie forward, "Go, Rosie, GO, GO, GO, GO!!" with each sweep of his cap in

the arc toward the finish line. On the homestretch, Rosie could see Joan next to her and heard severely labored breathing matching her own. Joan wasn't used to going to fast for so long. Could Rosie take her?

On the Baker track, out of turn 4, the Finish Line was still a LONG way away for a 200 meter sprinter. Rosie began to think maybe she could take her. As much as her lungs burned and her legs screamed, Rosie was not yet finished with her sprint. She was not fading. If she could maintain and Joan faded, the race would belong to her.

"Ride through the pain!" she had heard so often. "You can't win unless you're willing to hurt!"

She felt Joan collide with her briefly as they neared the finish. "She's trying to knock me down!" Rosie screamed to herself. "No more Ms Nice Guy!" and her anger added the adrenaline rush needed to take

her to the finish -- upright -- at full speed, and throw her bike across the line -- another move she had practiced endless times. She had no idea who finished first, she also knew not to look, to just give it everything she had. She'd have to see what the refs said. She felt good for the ride. It was good. It was what she could do. Whatever the outcome, it was good.

Dave came running up to her, "Great ride! That was such a good trick, it completely confused her because you didn't do what she expected. I'm so proud of you!"

"Thanks!" Rosie said, "I know it won't work next time, but I thought I'd try it."

"Great decision!" Dave said. "You must be a good strategist, like your dad."

"Yeah, just like my dad" Rosie smiled, feeling a little confused. Was he just projecting? Did he know her dad? Who was this guy?

Rosie rode to the warm-up track to cool down. Chilly was there and approached her.

"Hey, I still don't have a Madison partner, are you still looking for one too?" Chilly asked.

Hmph! Oh yeah, now that she had a good race, he's all enthusiastic now? Could she recover by tomorrow? She's have another sprint round tomorrow too. While she though she might be able to do it, she wasn't sure.

"Oh, I don't know, I'm not sure I'll ride it." Rosie replied coolly, really just too tired fresh from her race to look forward to another so soon, but lying. She was dying to ride it. But he'd insulted her, he could at least have given her a trial before discounting her abilities.

"Okay, well if you decide to, let me know." said Chilly, unsure of why she was so desperate before and now sounded so casual.

Women!

Joan joined Rosie on the warm up track, acknowledging her. She rode another warm-down lap, then rode beside her.

"That was a pretty good trick you pulled out there. I admit, I completely did NOT expect that. I had NO idea what you were doing! I thought you'd lost your mind. Plus, this track sucks! It's too long!"

"Not for me!" Rosie responded, laughing.

"Well let me warn you, that's the only way you won that one and next time it won't be so easy. It's two out of three, you know, and I intend to win."

"I understand" said Rosie, wallowing in her win, having no need to cause a fight or buck a challenge with anyone, not even her competition. She smiled and rode on. She was happy to win once. Joan did not look very happy -- in fact, she looked very pale.

Later that day, Rosie heard over the loud speaker that there would be no more competition for women's sprints, that one of the competitors had withdrawn from competition. Rosie looked over at Joan's tent only to see her lying down. She walked over.

"What's the matter?" she asked. Joan still looked pale and had a bucket next to her.

"I feel awful, Rosie. Really awful. I don't have any strength or energy and I feel like I'm going to throw up every minute, though I haven't done it yet. I just can't continue. I know I would have beat you if I wasn't sick." Joan insisted.

"Well, I don't know about that, but since you're so sick I'll agree with you." Rosie sympathized. "This is not the way I want to win. I like to think I could have beaten you."

"Well, I guess we'll have to wait for Natz *(National Championships)* to find out. Are you going?" Joan asked.

"You bet, I want a rematch!" Rosie kidded.

"I'll be up for it by then. I don't know if this is food poisoning or the flu, but I'm out for now. I hate to give you the prize money, but that's just what has to happen." Joan sighed.

"Great, I need some new wheels!" Rosie said, with a little smile. "I hope you feel better." And she waved goodbye.

On the way back to her tent, Rosie ran into Dave again.

"What happened?" he asked.

"She's sick. "Flu or food poisoning, she's not sure which." Rosie told him.

"Well you can still feel proud of your race, that was really great. Next time you'll beat her again. She probably dropped out so she wouldn't be humiliated. You really looked good out there, kiddo." Dave crowed. "Your dad is so proud of you."

"Do you know my dad?" Rosie asked.

"I sure do, are you kidding, we go WAY back." Dave replied.

"Are you one of those Little 500 guys?" she asked.

"Bingo!" said Dave.

"Oh, now I get it! Where is my dad?" Rosie asked.

Dave pointed "He's right over there... Oh wait, he was over there. I'm not sure where he is, but he's here, and so proud of you."

"Well if you see him before I do, let him know I'll come find him." Rosie instructed.

"Will do," said Dave, and walked toward the stands.

Mike and the Soldier's Cross - PTSD

"Did you see that? Your little girl! What a ride!" Dave exclaimed to Mike. He could see Mike's face was flushed with excitement. He must be very proud.

"That was incredible!" said Mike, "I couldn't believe it, and my

88

daughter, especially, how did she learn how to do that? I couldn't believe it!" he repeated. "Yeah, our Little 500 was exciting, but I never saw anything like this before, with the fake out and the sprinting -- it reminded me of football!"

"You have a lot to be proud of, she really did great." Dave said, sitting down next to Mike, still breathless from watching his girl. They were on turn three, where there were few people.

Dave had his eye on Cyril's daughter Marie, getting ready for the next race. They'd had some trouble with the starting pistols. This one was the Pursuit, and HAD to go off with starting pistols to start the race. They had to go off with precision, exactly when they were supposed to, or it completely messed up the race. Two misfires had happened twice already and it was hard on the riders to have to do restarts. This time they were determined to get it right. Darn starting pistols! Mike felt very unnerved, old horrors dancing before his eyes every time he heard a gun. Knowing it was coming didn't help.

Mike started talking about his time "in country" and about cautions with guns that happened in those days. You had to depend 100% that your gun would fire when you needed it to, and precisely the way you wanted it to. No second guessing in the military, especially the Marines. He lowered his voice, referring to fallen comrades.

"You hear about these things all the time, but you don't know what it's like unless you experience it. I've had a really hard time getting over some of the stuff I experienced, too awful to talk about. I never thought I'd be like this, but when I looked over and saw my buddy Gabe with half his head missing, it was like the most horrible dream you can ever have. It's like it's not real, but so awful that in a millisecond you are never the same again. The worst thing is that I should have stopped it, I should have saved him. It was my fault!"

"That sounds terrible, Mike, I'm sorry you had to go through that." responded Dave. "I hope they get this starting gun stuff settled, I hate to hear them over and over, too."

Mike was bent over, elbows on his knees, looking at the ground, remembering the worst moment in his life and the loss of his best friend in the Corps. Dave, while sympathetic, was watching the riders, watching Marie nervously waiting for the officials to make sure their pistols would work predictably this time. A shot nearby rang out, followed almost immediately by another shot on the other side.

Dave suddenly felt himself grabbed and thrown to the ground, under the seats, with Mike on top of him. Mike was shaking, and had a strong hold on Dave, covering his head, almost suffocating him. Dave couldn't move. Mike was a big, muscular guy, still in military shape, even though he was now in his 50s. Dave was still the slim, in-shape guy he'd always been, but he was pretty much unable to move under weight and strength. What was wrong with Mike?

"Mike, What are you doing? Get off!" Dave said, "Get up!?"

Mike was in obvious distress. "I've got you!" he yelled "Not this time, NOT this time!" He was still shaking, his eyes glazed, and not letting Dave up. "Not this time" he muttered again. "Not this time"...

"Mike!" Dave yelled at him, with no response, even though Mike's ear was 6 inches from his mouth. "Mike!" he yelled again.

Mike still had a glazed look in his eyes. Dave had never seen him that way. Then Mike's face cleared up and he looked at Dave, inches from his eyes.

"Oh my god... !" and he started to cry softly. Mike, big tough Mike, started to cry. Dave couldn't look away -- he still couldn't move -- he watched Mike collapse into an emotional state he had never seen. It wasn't anger. It wasn't violence, It was fear. It was a deep, forlorn heartache, collapsing into an inconsolable, hopeless anguish. Mike rolled

over and let him up, but stayed down himself for a few more minutes, sobbing. Dave realized that Mike had brought with him internal damage from a life that Dave hadn't shared. Luckily, no one was sitting close enough to see what had happened.

"Mike, is there anything I can do?" Dave asked. Mike kept his head down, trying to get in control of himself. A grown man collapsing into a little baby in front of all of these people was not an image Mike wanted to convey. This situation was completely embarrassing and humiliating. Mike didn't think he could get up. He stayed down. Dave was always such an understanding guy.

"What is it, Mike?" Dave asked. "What is it?"

"I didn't expect this to happen here", admitted Mike. "I've been to counseling and had meds to work it out. I've worked on it so hard. I thought I could come here and not have this happen, but I didn't expect the guns. That just set it all off again. A lot of the guys have similar problems, but they don't help us. I've been taking meds for years, but I still have nightmares. It's the weirdest thing, Dave, I start thinking it's gone and all of a sudden it just GRABS me, and there's nothing I can do to control it. It's like a seizure, and I keep thinking it's gone and take the meds they give me, and as much as I think I've got control of it, it hits me again and again. Sometimes I just feel like giving up, like I can't take it any more."

"Mike, I'm so sorry." Dave said quietly. "I had no idea. You know, there's a guy who works with me that told me some things."

His voice trailed off, but, like the many unspoken understandings Mike and Dave had always had, he knew that even though Dave hadn't shared the experience, he empathized with loss and sorrow and many of the other sadnesses that life brings with it. Dave looked at him, recovering for some minutes, then decided he'd do the only thing he could think of to make Mike feel better -- or at least distract him from his heartache.

"I'm going to tell you something I didn't want to tell anyone, Mike. I had eight years of really great racing with CinZano, the camaraderie, the victories, the defeats... it brought us together, not like war, of course, but in a similar spiritual way. You never forget those things you experience so closely and with such a HUGE impact on who you are. Those things I understand. What I still keep as my big dark secret is the hard times I went through when the racing was coming to a close and I knew I'd be cut from the team and all the experiences that you have when you're at the top. I went into a severe depression that lasted a couple of years. Since I worked for CinZano, I had access to a lot of liquor. If I wasn't drinking a martini, I was drinking a Manhattan. If I wasn't drinking a sweet Vermouth, I was drinking a dry Vermouth -- just making sure to expand my palate, you understand. Then there were all the competitors brands that I had to taste-compare and the wide variety of flavorings, I swallowed more than I should have — way more than I spit out, which is what I should have done."

"I was only doing it for my job, you understand. I learned that I'm not a happy drunk, I'm a mean drunk. I'm surprised Joelle didn't leave me, but she grew up in Europe, she understood, and put up with what was wrong, hoping I'd "grow" out of it. She knew why, she knew how much I missed riding and being part of the team. She knew there were a lot of pressures on me at work. It's not unusual for people in the liquor industry to have problems with liquor, when the things get tough, there's a nice handy solution available. We see it all the time. The smart ones stop drinking, or at least learn how to taste without losing control. The dumb ones lose control. Which one was I?"

"Well, I was the dumb one for a while, until my dad came to visit. You know, that old guy, as cranky as he was, he set me straight. I used to think he didn't understand anything, but he understands alcoholism. He grew up with an uncle who he loved very much, that the family lost to alcoholism. He watched it growing up and told me how he felt when the old guy passed out on some railroad tracks one night on the way home, and got hit by a train. The pain I saw and his plain talk made me look at myself. I didn't like what I saw. I just got lost. I got back in my bike, and after a few hundred miles I straightened my life out -- well, mostly, anyway."

"I know it isn't the same as what happened to you, Mike, but it's something that embarrasses me to the point where I had to make some real life changes to recover my self-respect and see how good life can be. I wasn't going to tell anyone that story, but there it is. My life isn't perfect either."

Mike looked at Dave. He could see that Dave had summoned all his courage up to try and make him feel better, reliving a painful and humiliating memory, in order to help him. Well, friends do stuff like that.

"I guess none of us turned out perfect, huh? I wonder how Cyril and Moocher did. Of all of us, I would have pegged Moocher of having the crummiest life, but he and Nancy seem so happy." commented Mike.

"Yeah, he does," Dave replied. "Maybe we should have stayed in Bloomington."

Just then, Cyril lumbered up.

"What are you guys doing over here?" he asked. "Why aren't you at the other end of the track with everyone else?"

Cyril had been watching the officials trying to get their guns working properly and organize riders. Riders had been given a break until they were ready.

"We were just talking," said Dave. "Talking about the good old days, catching up some of the time in between."

Mike looked at Dave for some sign that Dave would expose his "secret". Dave looked back, straight faced. Good old Dave. He was such a monstrously good friend.

"Well, I sure hope you guys have had better luck than me," said Cyril. "I've been plagued by crazy administrators, students wanting grades for doing nothing, demands for research that costs money at the same time they're making huge budget cuts. Melody's been passed over again and again for the Department Chair job -- I swear it's just because she's so beautiful -- they never look at how brilliant she is! It's been HELL trying to be a college professor and survive in that poisonous atmosphere!"

Dave and Mike took their eyes away from Cyril. They understood that we all have our burdens and life damages us, then throws us out for more, but they didn't have the heart to replay the heart-wrenching true life confessions they'd just been through. They were exhausted.

Then Mike started to smirk. He caught Dave's eye and Dave couldn't help but understand what he was thinking.

"Gee, that's terrible, Cyril. It sounds like you've been through some heavy stuff!" he said.

He looked at Dave again. Dave couldn't control a smile. That turned into a full grin. Dave looked back at Mike. Mike started to laugh. Dave started to laugh, too. One built upon the other until both were in hysterical, stomach-wrenching, breath-defying peals of full-on, out-of-control laugher. Their eyes watered. Their laughter turned into near-sobs, they could not control. Mike dropped to the ground, laughter continuing for several minutes, reveling in the joy of joy. It felt so much better than fear and grief. Mike knew he'd made the right choice in coming to the bike race in spite of his fear of exactly what had happened. He'd hoped for acceptance, but this was reliving the best of the old times they had enjoyed, when he was so often angry, but had a few of these laugh sessions too. Every time he and Dave started to stop laughing, they'd catch each others' eyes again and would start up again. Cyril was completely perplexed.

"Hey, what's so funny?" he asked. "I mean it, it's tough out there, you guys have no idea what I've had to put up with!"

Dave gasped, "We're not laughing at you, Cyril, I'm sorry, we're just happy to be back together."

"Yeah, Cyril, we're just so happy to see you again!" gulped Mike.

This statement was so absurd, considering the source of the hysterical laugher, that it set them both off again, and they fell into wails of hilarity. By this time, partly due to laughter's contagion and partly due to the absurdity of Mike's pronouncement, Cyril had to join in, until they were all three howling with enjoyment. He'd missed them much more than he'd realized.

It didn't matter why they were laughing, it just felt good.

"Let's go eat." Mike said.

5. The Madison

Chilly walked over to Rosie again after she'd warmed down. He was still impressed, she looked really good out there, like she knew what she was doing. Carrying on a long sprint after surprising Joan was impressive. Rosie was obviously not a new rider. Just because he didn't remember her from other events didn't mean much; he knew practiced riders when he saw them. She did that sprint with a lot of confidence. He had seen Joan race against some top talent, and she was good. Beating her was an achievement, plus, Chilly liked the snap and endurance he saw in Rosie. Maybe she'd do as a partner. He wanted to race enough to swallow his pride and ask her, since no one else appeared available who had any experience in the Madison. Recognizing his own desperation, he assured himself that he was not just asking her because of that. He wanted to win! He knew who Shaun Wallace and Eddie B were, and he knew that both of them were World level coaches. Rosie had to have learned a tremendous amount from them. The fact that she trained with both when she could, was also impressive. Both of them trained women and trained riders in the Madison. He'd have to try her out, though, to make sure Rosie could give a good handsling, enough to actually propel him into the race when they switched race segments. He wanted a partner, not a figurehead. He thought she might feel a little more recovered now.

"Do you have a partner for the Madison yet?" he persisted.

"No, I'm not going to do it." she replied, with finality.

"What? I thought you wanted to, wanted to bad. I'm good at Madison, it's one of my best events, we could win! Even if I just rode it alone, I think I could win it." Chilly boasted.

Was he kidding? She didn't know if he realized what he was implying -- that he didn't really need a partner. She took it personally, knowing that he would probably not say that to a guy.

"No, I don't feel like it any more. I'm tired from that last race. I don't think I'll recover by tomorrow." she lied, insulted at his implication.

"Sure you will. Come on, give it a try, I'll teach you anything you need to know." Chilly insisted.

"Oh, really?" responded Rosie irritated, "You'll teach me a few things? Don't bother bud, I'm probably not up to your high standards, anyway."

"Hey, I didn't mean to insult you, it's just that I love the Madison, it's probably my favorite race. I've learned a few things and I'm willing to share some techniques..." Chilly said hopefully.

"Well that's great, but I'm fine. You go ahead with someone you think is worthy. I'll watch." said Rosie, with more finality. She walked away to look for her dad.

It took her a full turn of the track to find him, but at last she saw her dad, sitting in turn 3. He looked really tired, and two of his "brothers" were sitting with him, one of them the guy who had been her holder. Oh yeah, she thought, I can see how they looked in that old photograph, there they are, okay. As she approached, Cyril and Dave got up.

"We're going over to get some snacks, they said to Rosie. Want anything, Mike?" Dave asked.

"Nah, I'm good, maybe later." but as they walked a few steps later, he called after them.

"Hey, wait!" they turned. "On the other hand, surprise me!" and he settled down to talk to his girl.

"Wow, that was a great race you rode, honey. I was so proud of you! Cyril and I aren't as up on how those things happen, but Dave told us he suggested you try and surprise her from farther out, and I guess she was surprised!" he crowed.

"Yeah, well, she was trying to force me up toward the rail and I already knew that she thought I'd cooperate and go up track. If she had been able to get to the top, she'd have been able to gain more speed on the banking, so the higher I was and the less banking she had to start her sprint, the better. She was a little too predictable in her "head turns" to see where I was behind her, I could almost time the turns like a metronome. I knew exactly when she would turn left to look for me, so it was easier then I thought to trick her. The trouble is, it won't be so easy next time. Now she knows I can beat her. But I know it too!" Rosie exclaimed.

Mike didn't fully understand what she was talking about, but he wasn't even really listening, he was just so proud of her. If Dave said it was a great move, he knew it was. His little girl...

"This guy Chilly wanted me to do the Madison with him, but I put him in his place. He insulted me! He wanted me to partner him after seeing my sprint and then he acted like it would be some big honor to be his partner in the Madison, like I'd never done them before, like he knew everything and I knew nothing. I'm a good Madison rider, dad. Why do guys always make those assumptions, that THEY know and just because I'm a girl, I don't? I turned him down, he can just go find someone else to listen to his big head." she pouted.

Mike recognized the name immediately. He knew Chilly was Moocher's kid and the thought of watching the two kids together sounded like a lot of fun. He didn't care who would win, he didn't even know what a Madison was. He recognized the arrogant Chilly in her description. Nancy had written that one of the reasons Chilly was so good was because he had a tendency to brag and then practically killed himself to live up to what he had bragged about. Mike recognized that kind of thing in himself, too, so it sounded familiar. It wasn't easy to do that. He liked the kid already.

"What would you need to do as his partner, Rosie?" he asked her.

"Well, let me explain the Madison. It's an old race that started in

Madison Square Garden where the riders would race for six days in a row. That's why they fall it a "Madison". I think it started during the Depression. Anyway, now it's part of Nationals, but sometimes they have special events with it."

"Each team has two riders who are partners. They start the race with half the riders on the track and half the riders on the fence. Once the race starts, they trade off racing. One rider sprints while the other one rests."

"The most important thing is you have to learn," she continued, "is how to do the exchanges, where one person grabs the other's hand and throws them into the race. So it's not like you just ride your bike fast. You have to know where to be, so you don't get into crashes.You have to be able to sprint and you have to have good endurance, because it's always a long race. It used to be just for guys, but now women race it too. It's really fun!" Rosie explained.

Rosie went silent, looking across the field at Chilly, who was walking among the tents. She figured he was still looking for a partner. It was tempting to run across the track while they were between sessions and tell him she'd do it, but she was still mad.

Mike always enjoyed sharing with his brothers and this would be pretty special.

"Why don't you do it? It sounds like a fun race!" he asked.

"No, I decided he could just have his ego, I didn't want anything to do with it." Rosie explained. "He had his chance to be nice to me and not act like a jerk, but he blew it! And more than once! It really made me mad."

Mike was quiet for a few minutes, watching her watch Chilly. He loved his girl so much, and wished he could have back the years he was gone from her. He felt lucky to see her involved in a fun and healthy activity. He thought of how cool it would be if his girl and Moocher's boy raced together, for all of them. They might even win! He knew that Chilly had a good reputation for winning, especially the longer races. He saw a chance to impart some of his best advice to his little girl, advice that she might not listen to otherwise.

"Rosie, I see he hurt your pride, but let me give you some advice from your old dad. Don't pass by opportunities that might be fun or good for you, just because of pride, I did that and it caused me trouble my whole life".

Mike recalled that he almost didn't come to the race, he was so afraid of exactly what had happened, humiliation in front of his "brothers". He never knew when the PTSD would overwhelm him, so he had withdrawn from several activities because he was so afraid of revealing his vulnerability.

But this was not about him. This was about his girl, and he had just learned what was most important from what had just happened. Even though it was his worst fear (these days), missing the opportunity to watch his little girl race would have been even worse.

"I've just learned that pride really isn't important. Friendships are what's important in life. Pride only holds you back from enjoying life to the fullest. Make new friends when you can, and I'll bet this Chilly kid could be a great friend to you -- you know, once you straighten him out on your abilities and he knows you are someone to reckon with."

Mike went silent, then added, "Think about it."

"Okay, dad." was all she said in response. "I guess I'll go get my gear together. I'm really tired." and she walked back across the track to her tent.

Meanwhile, Chilly was really depressed he didn't have a Madison partner. He had a GREAT guy partner, why did they have to change it to co-ed? He'd ridden Madisons with girls before and he knew it was possible they knew how to do it, but he was so good at it, why didn't this Rosie girl understand that he wanted to give her a gift of his knowledge. She would be so lucky, and she didn't seem to know it! He wondered if maybe she had already ridden enough of them to be as good a partner as he had been looking for. He saw Shaun Wallace sitting with the San Diego contingent in a tent near the officials stand. He walked over and introduced himself.

"Mr Wallace... they call me "Chilly"" he started...

"Hi, Chilly, you can call me Shaun." Shaun responded. "What can I do for you?" he asked.

"Well, you know Rosie, a rider at your track?" Chilly asked.

"Sure, she's one of our best up-and-coming riders." he answered.

"I don't mean this the way it sounds, but is she very good at the Madison?"

"Absolutely", he answered, "she's been working on it for a couple of years, and she's gotten pretty good at it, why do you ask?" Shaun questioned.

"Well, I asked her to partner with me and she got all insulted when I told her I'd share some of my best moves with her." Chilly explained.

Shaun laughed. "Yup, that's our Rosie. She's kind of hot-headed, but that's partly just the way she is. Have you ever met her dad? She's a chip off the old block. I've told her many times to just pour that passion into her racing and it has helped her win several races just because she gets insulted. I'll tell you a little secret about her: Imply that she might not be able to do it and it gets her blood up. You'll get the best performance out of her that she has -- maybe even better than you think possible." he confided.

"Actually, I think I already did that." Chilly laughed. "I questioned her because I want a partner who can race, not one who will bungle the exchange and knock everybody down. The last thing I want to do is either knock her down or have her get in my way. She got pretty mad." Chilly admitted.

"Well no problem there", Shaun said. "I taught her how to stay out of the way and plan for the exchange well before it's time, if possible. You know how Madisons are, everyone's trying to race and exchange, so it can be pretty hectic, but she understands exchanges, and she's gotten good at the handsling. She puts her whole body into it, and she's a good bike handler. She races with the men and the women in San Diego because she's that good. She holds her own in the co-ed Madison races too, she's won a few, depending on who her partner was. Rosie's pretty dependable, it's usually her partner who is the wild card for winning or losing. If you're a good Madison rider, I'd say you two have a good chance."

Before Shaun had even finished his feedback, Chilly was convinced that Rosie might be his best possibility for winning the race. He wished he'd gone a little easier on her and gave her more credit for possibly being a good rider, it's just that the Madison is less common at some tracks and the fact is, many men weren't good at the exchanges either, and if you couldn't stay out of the way and couldn't do a good handsling, the rest of the riders really didn't want you in the race. Accidents ruined it for everyone. He thought she would understand why he underestimated her, but apparently she just got mad. Okay, he'd have to try a different approach. He'd act like she knows everything and see where that goes. He'd have to act humble -- which for him was strictly an act.

When he approached Rosie this time, it was with great caution. His options were running out, and she might be his best chance to have a good race. He walked slowly toward her, trying to display a conciliatory smile.

"Hi, I just thought I'd check back to see..."

"Oh hi," she turned at the sound of his voice. "If you haven't found a partner yet, I'll ride with you, but remember, I'm your partner, not your sidekick."

What?? He thought this would be a tough sell, but now, all of a sudden, she was willing to just hop on the train? He would never understand women. What happened to change her mind? That was okay, he wouldn't question it.

"The race is tomorrow," she added, "did you want to practice a few handslings tonight after racing is over? We'd better see if we can even make a good team."

"Okay, what time?" he asked, surprised, but wishing to offer her power in their decisions.

"I think everything will be done around five. Let's meet then. We can practice for an hour or two, then still have time to eat and go to bed early." she proposed. "I want to get a LOT of sleep, it's a long race."

"Works for me." he said simply, with a relieved smile. He walked away, shaking his head slowly.

Women!

5 pm Handsling Practice

When they met for practice, they were both on time and ready to go. Chilly took this as a good sign. At least she didn't stop to comb her hair or some stupid thing like that. They both climbed on their bikes and slowly circled the track.

"So do you want to be Cav or Wiggo?" Rosie asked.

"What?" Chilly asked, not sure he understood what she meant.

"Do you want to be Cav or Wiggo?" Rosie insisted.

"What do you mean?" asked Chilly again, not quite sure she knew what she was implying. Did she know who those guys were?

"Did you watch the 2016 World Madison race?" she asked.

"Well of course!" he said.

"So, you know, Cavendish and Wiggins, 2016 Madison Champs. Cav is the sprinter, Wiggins is the endurance rider. Do you have a better sprint or endurance? I like to imagine I'm some World class rider. It usually helps me in my races. I just focus on that person and do what I saw that person do. Lately I've watched Sarah Hammer a lot, and it's really helped me. She is so great, sprint or endurance. It really helped me to imagine I'm her during my races, but I haven't seen her race a Madison, so I'll have to channel Cav or Wiggo." she repeated.

Hmmm not a bad idea, Chilly thought. If he admitted it, when he watched Worlds, he often found himself imagining a performance like he was watching and it helped him plan strategies to watch what others did, like Peter Sagan, when he went off the front and won the 2015 World Road race. That was a big gamble, but it paid off for Sagan. He was known as having a great sprint and great endurance, just the kind of rider Chilly wanted to be -- and had been able to be a couple of times.

"Oh, okay," Chilly responded. "Good idea. What do you think?"

He thought he'd be as agreeable as he could be so as not to insult her again.

"I can do either. What about Andy and Sheryl? Do you know them?" she asked.

"Yes, I've run into them several times, never in a Madison. Each is a pretty good all-around rider, but I think I'd better be Cav, because Andy is a good sprinter and I have more testosterone than you, so we might be a better match." he smiled.

"Okay, I'll be Wiggo. Just don't overlap wheels and crash during the race like Cav did, "Cav"." she smiled so he would know she was just joking. "I think Sheryl and I are pretty equal as riders, though I've never seen her in a Madison."

"I don't overlap wheels." he responded. She could hear the "testiness" in his voice this time.

But he didn't want her to change her mind and decide not to race with him, so he quickly recovered.

"I'm just kidding!" and then he took what he knew was a risk. "I checked with Shaun about you and he had nothing but good things to say." he admitted.

"Oh really?" her voice getting testy again.

"Look Rosie," he said quietly, "it's nothing against you, I have the same hesitancy with you that I'd have pairing up with a new guy. We haven't raced together before and we're all the way across the country from each other, so I'm just being cautious. You should be too."

"Okay," she answered, "Let's try this out and see if we can actually do the deed."

"Okay," he said, "two more laps warmup and let's try a couple of exchanges."

"Okay," she repeated.

"I tend to try to do exchanges on the back straight if I can, just because it's flatter and it seems like there's a little less congestion. Let's start there." Chilly proposed. "Next lap."

As they came around toward turn two, Rosie slowed and rode to the top of the track to wait. Chilly accelerated gradually into the far turns, three and four, planning on staying at the bottom of the track, to wait for her to catch him for the exchange, as he would during a race -- if she could catch him! He didn't accelerate fully to give her a chance to catch him. Coming into turn one, he maintained speed, waiting to see if she could catch up. As he rode into turn two, she dropped down, accelerating quickly, pulling along side, grabbing his hand. He took hold and pulled her forward gently, continuing the handsling until they were too far apart to touch each other. He heard her yelling from the front of him.

"Hey, don't go easy on me, don't treat me like I'm a girl -- THROW me!" she shouted. "I need your help to get up to speed!"

Fine, he thought, we'll see how you do next time, little girl... and he slowed, riding to the top of turns three and four, waiting for her to come around. As she approached, he rode down the banking, matching her speed to come along side her. She reached out, grabbed his hand, twisting her body, but keeping her bike straight, pulling hard and throwing him forward.

Holy cow, she really CAN throw! he thought. For an instant, he almost lost his balance it was so unexpected, but he recovered quickly. Maybe this would work after all.

For the rest of the practice, they exchanged over and over, getting used to the "feel" of each other. A couple of times they missed, or only touched. They had to get used to each others' style, but it didn't seem nearly as far off as each expected. In fact, it was almost familiar.

Shaun taught Rosie how to exchange the same way he'd teach any guy, no light-weight, delicate "girlie" throws. She could really throw, and she knew to maintain her line, not wobbling to connect or wobbling more to pull and throw. Over and over she reached for Chilly's hand, relaxing into his pull and throw, then immediately accelerating back into the invisible race. This would work. Or, at least, Chilly concluded that he had as good a chance with this new partner as he had with any other women he'd raced with. By the end of their practice they flowed. Each felt happy and comfortable with the other.

What a relief, Chilly thought. And I almost didn't ask her again. Mom and dad always said, "Persistence is the key to success."

Once they called it quits for the night, they gathered up their gear. Moocher was waiting, and Mike sauntered over. Both dads had been watching the last portion of the practice.

"Hey, your little girl looked pretty good!" Moocher said to Mike as they hugged hello. Chilly and Rosie both rolled their eyes as they looked at each other.

"Oh yeah, well, your boy looked pretty good. I might trust him with my little girl. She's pretty good, just like her old man."

Moocher laughed. Same old Mike.

"I don't know how this happened," said Moocher, "but it sure will be fun to have them race together."

"I'll come find you tomorrow," Mike replied. "Cyril and Dave will be here. That will be a great race for us all to watch together."

"See you here!" called Moocher as he helped Chilly carry off his gear. He called back: "Where are we going to meet? On the backstretch?"

"Over there," called Mike, pointing toward the backstretch, not really sure where "the backstretch" was, as he hoisted Rosie's bike on his shoulder and grabbed extra wheels.

"Want me to carry anything else?" he asked her, reaching for her bag.

She sighed. Typical dad, when it came to lifting stuff.

"No, I've got it." she said, pulling one bag on her shoulder and the other in her hand. The bags looked really heavy, so he insisted they trade burdens. She argued for a minute, but then realized how much he wanted to feel like a dad, so she agreed. Once she had the bike on her shoulder and wheels in her hand, he was surprised at the heaviness of her bags.

"That bike weighs nothing. Way lighter than in my day. These bags are heavy!" he exclaimed.

"Yeah, that's why I do weights." she kidded.

That's my girl! thought Mike, seeing her independence. They turned and walked to Mike's Jeep Renegade.

Impress Them

The guys finally got together on the outside of the track. Dave and Moocher made sure their kids were set up, then hopped over the track rail. They loved this track for the same reason they'd loved the Little 500 track. They could see everything, just like all tracks, all the excitement. It was great being together again, just like in the old days.

They could also see who had the most expensive car (Dave, with his Range Rover) and who had the least expensive car (Moocher, with his old VW bus), but that was pretty much the way it had always been, so it wasn't much of a surprise. They were even surprised Moocher HAD a car. Cyril's car was a larger model Japanese sedan, suitable for a college professor. Mike had an older model Jeep Renegade. He only admitted within himself that he partly picked it for the name. His brothers already knew that.

Now that they were men, with decades passing since their days together in Bloomington, each "boy" wanting to impress the other with his status, his children, and his position in life. Dave was the most obviously successful. His expensive running shoes and casually exotic gear told all of them he was money. He didn't act any different toward the others than he ever did, but they were still aware of his success. He saw each of them as successes too. The military appeared to do Mike a huge favor with his experience of status, a life of discipline, and a tight regimen that he understood. He seemed happy and willing to expound on the glories of international travel and manly expression of saving the nation. The Marines agreed with him. Even his brother Steve had to admit that he was a changed man. What no one except Dave knew was the Big Secret of PTSD Mike carried with him every day, uncertain when it would rear its ugly head and expose his weakness. In fact, he was terrified of his own vulnerability. It was the LAST thing he wanted the others to find out about. He was always the driver, the one in command! But now Dave knew, and that put Mike at ease. It really wouldn't matter if all of them knew now. He figured Dave might tell them, but Mike didn't want to talk about it. He'd leave it up to Dave.

Cyril loved the others' reaction to his wife Melody. He should be used to it by now, but he hadn't seen THEIR reactions yet. Their eyes got big, they stumbled over their words and were transfixed by her, just like everyone else. Once they were alone, they all wanted to know by what magic plain old Cyril had attracted such a beauty. Cyril?!? He never looked for the beautiful chicks or tried to date the glamor girls. What gives?

"I know, guys, I know. But you know, really and truly, she and I didn't start out as a couple, we were just working on papers together online, I never knew what she looked like, and I found out she has a brilliant mind! When I actually MET her, I had the same reaction, but then I forgave her for being beautiful." and he laughed. "Now she's just 'Mel'".

He always laughed (within himself) about her ability to stun, because he could see it, but only intellectually, now. Somehow, beautiful women had never interested him. Maybe he thought they were meant for other men, he recognized that, psychologically, it might be rationalization, but it was her inner beauty that always captivated him. He still enjoyed it when men reacted to her as though they'd just been tasered and lost the ability to talk. He thought that was funny. She was even more overwhelming when she wore high heels -- he had no idea how she could wear such things, but he'd gotten used to them. He used one to open an oil can one time. They almost raised her up close enough to kiss her. He thought that was what they were for.

Meanwhile, Moocher was obviously a thoroughly happy man. He was a great dad, he and Nancy were extremely close and the kids were all well behaved. Everyone in the "Moocher" Mullins family seemed happy to help each other, almost like they could read each others' minds. It was pretty impressive. The boys had noticed it in Bloomington, but they were almost jealous now that they saw that it had lasted all these years, even though Moocher and Nancy still never had any money. They all sort of felt sorry for him, but he seemed so content, all they could feel was happy for him.

After Mike's response to the Starter's pistol, some truths began

emerging. The dam burst and the boys shared their inner-most secrets --
if they had any. The most obvious was Mike's PTSD. Moocher and Dave
hadn't known people who had been so damaged by war, but Cyril had
studied it as a part of his studies. He understood what happened to Mike
and had counseled a couple of vets who had returned from war. He had
seen some pretty damaged men and helped them get connected with
services. Mike had twice attempted really hard to get help, but not with
anyone who truly knew what he'd been through and what he needed.

Cyril offered all services and assistance at his disposal to Mike. If
nothing else, it made Mike feel much better, sort of like he had his own
personal doctor. Plus, he'd "have to" go to Colorado, with all those
glorious mountains, where he always felt the most peace. Mike hated the
look on Moocher's face when he listened to what happened. Moocher
wanted so much to help, but he had no idea how or what to do. But, Mike
knew Moocher was on his side, no matter what.

The guys walked back to the track to watch their children get
back to their racing. Cyril's daughter Marie was racing, but it was more
in theory than in practice. She loved to ride the track, but really didn't
care much about winning. She just liked the fun of riding and
competition gave her a reason to ride faster and harder. Otherwise, she
was fine just riding for health and camaraderie. Cyril and Melody were
happy that she was happy, so that worked for them, too.

The Morning of the Race

Chilly and Rosie warmed up on the track and on their rollers
(stationary trainers), setting them up near each other. Their tents weren't
that far apart. They warmed up while other races went on. In between
races, they tried a few exchanges as others practiced theirs. Chilly saw a
distinct danger, and it wasn't him and Rosie. It was Andy and Sheryl.
Their exchanges were not polished, and Sheryl didn't seem comfortable
executing them, though she was a good rider. After the night before,
Chilly half expected Andy and Sheryl to be as polished as he and Rosie
had become, but they clearly weren't. Now he doubted they had
practiced. Plus, Andy was yelling at Sheryl, which didn't help her
performance. They didn't look like they were exactly sure about what
they were doing.

Partnering is a wild card even when it's not co-ed. Some partners
just flow together, like he and Rosie had flowed. He was very surprised
how easily they had learned to anticipate each other's moves and

strength. She seemed ready for his grasp and he ready for hers. They had progressively developed increased confidence in each other's ability to first, connect, and then throw with force, enough force to actually propel the other rider, and not slow down. She practiced looking around before going up track, even though there were no other riders there. She had enough "snap" to catch up with him and to accelerate into his throw. This would work.

But Sheryl seemed hesitant, and more than once she started to pull up track into the path of another rider who was accelerating to catch her partner. This could be dangerous.

Andy was a strong rider, as strong as Chilly, and Chilly knew how much he wanted to win. The last thing any of them wanted to do was go down in a crash. If Sheryl, through no fault of her own, was not practiced enough to perform near his level, it endangered all riders in the field.

Chilly walked over to let Andy know that he was a little uncomfortable with their team.

"Hey Andy, have you and Sheryl partnered in Madison before?" asked Chilly.

Andy knew the truth of what he was implying, but, like Chilly, he almost couldn't find a partner, so he was thrilled to just be in the race. Like Chilly, he figured he could really practically win by riding solo. For him a woman partner was somewhat inconvenient, but he figured he'd win because he was one of the best riders on the track and Chilly knew he thought this. Andy thought the race would really be between him and Chilly. For Andy, the girls were just decoration. Chilly could see that some of the Seattle riders were also fast and experienced, but all of them had been forced to suddenly make new plans by the sudden switch to a co-ed race, so some riders were fine with it, while others were unnerved by the change.

"Don't worry about it, Chilly man," Andy responded, icily. "We'll do great. You haven't ridden with Rosie before either have you? We're as prepared as you are."

Chilly wondered if Andy had watched as he and Rosie actually did the exchange and if he had the least concern for anyone else on the track. Apparently he cared about neither. Chilly decided that getting into a fight with Andy right before the race was a bad idea, so he decided to drop it. Both of them were lucky to have found partners at all at that very last minute. He could understand Andy overlooking Sheryl's obvious inexperience because she was fast.

At least he himself had a partner who seemed able and experienced at the throws. Now if they could just maintain speed over the whole 80 laps.

"Don't worry about us, Chilly man, we'll be in front of you!" called Andy after him as Chilly walked away.

"That's exactly what I'm worried about." Chilly mumbled to himself. Well, he also reasoned that sometimes fear could produce a better performance. Chilly already learned that that anger could produce a good performance. He was angry with Andy. Add fear, and his best performance might come out. He wasn't just apprehensive for himself, but also for Rosie and other riders. While he had become convinced that she could take care of herself, a rider who has little confidence in a crowd was dangerous, no matter who they were, and that's what he saw in Sheryl. It wasn't the pack riding, she was fine there, it was the exchanges. Well, there was nothing he could do but hope that his anger with Andy would win them the race. He'd need to warn Rosie. He found her taking a break from her rollers.

"Hey" he said as he approached.

"Hey" she responded.

"Have you been watching the other riders?" he asked.

"Yes," she replied. "Some of them are really good!"

"Have you noticed any who aren't so good?" he asked.

"Well, yeah, a couple. That girl Sheryl almost crashed another rider, but I only saw that once." she said.

"Yeah, well I've been watching her with Andy, too. Andy is someone I know really well and he has no problem with causing problems for other riders, especially if he thinks it can help him win. I don't trust him, and she scares me. It's not her fault, it's knowing that he will not care if she knocks anyone down or crashes herself. He'll probably just yell at her." he advised.

"Okay, thanks for the warning. She's a pretty nice girl, I've raced with her and she is a good rider. I've never seen her ride a Madison though. I'll be careful. Thanks for the heads up." Rosie returned to her rollers.

"My dad told me some things about your dad, by the way," Chilly added.

"So?!" Rosie said defensively.

Chilly laughed. "No, nothing bad, just that he was a top athlete, that he was a tough Marine, and that his daughter seemed a lot like him. Bullheaded." he added, smiling at her. "Really, I won't underestimate you again."

Rosie took the implied apology and praise for her dad as solid compliments. She was proud of her dad and always loved to be compared with him, as much as she loved her mom. Plus, Chilly seemed to be accepting her as an equal now, which is all she wanted.

"We'll probably be up in about a half hour. See you at the start line. Do you need anything?" he asked Rosie.

"No, I'm as ready as I'll ever be." she answered.

Chilly started to walk away. She called after him. "Chilly!"

He turned, surprised at her sudden softness.

"Thanks for persisting, for getting me to race. I would have been really bummed to watch all these other riders and not know what a good team we would have made." she said.

"Me too. Besides, our dads had never raced together before they won the 500, either." he said warmly.

She smiled a big, happy smile. He hoped he would see that same smile after the race, too.

The Madison Race

Rosie and Chilly approached the start line with a mixture of apprehension and excitement. It wasn't so much about winning yet, it

was much more about fitting in and having a good race -- and not going down in some crash. Rosie saw Andy, Chilly's arch-enemy, lined up in front of them. Rosie grabbed onto Chilly's bars to settle herself and wait for the roll-out as he held on to the rail. Her challenge would be in competing with Sheryl who was beside Andy. That was great, it would be Rosie against Sheryl, Chilly against Andy. Sheryl was from Minnesota. Even though they had one of the most beautiful and competitive tracks in the U.S. in Blaine, their racing program had gone through some rebuilding years, and was just getting back on its feet. It had gotten so bad that it appeared they might even close the track until a ground-swell of local bicycling enthusiasts got together to prevent that from happening. Sheryl was a great road rider, smart and strong. The track was not her forte but she was strong. She looked very fit and had won the Pursuit event, but she also looked tense and nervous. Rosie knew that Andy viewed himself as part of an unbeatable team, but that's not what Rosie thought when she looked at Sheryl's demeanor. Andy didn't know Rosie at all, so he probably figured Chilly would have no chance with an unknown rider. He barely looked at her. His eyes were on Chilly.

Hmph, that's what he thinks, she thought. "better if he underestimates me, anyway."

Once they were lined up, Madame Official (Rosie and Chilly called her, jokingly, because she was all about business and so in command) gave all riders a quick review of how the start would take place, the number of laps and sprints, and other useful information for the Madison specifically. Not too much information, just enough to refresh the memories of riders who were so excited that they might need a quick reminder of what they should already know. She knew that the riders' brains were fogged with excitement.

The announcer read off the list of teams for the crowds, noting where each team was from. "TeamSEA, from Seattle" got huge applause, then "Team DyMinn from Indy and Minnesota (Andy and Sheryl), Team IcyRose from Indy and San Diego" (Chilly and Rosie), Kissena... and down the list. Each was applauded by the audience, with Team SEA receiving the biggest applause as the hometown team. 16 teams altogether, 32 riders on the track, all grabbing and throwing each other forward every two laps. A twenty mile sprint. This could be dangerous -- and exciting! Madame Official gave her last minute reminder:

"Riders, you have 80 laps and 8 sprints, one sprint every 10 laps. This is an exhibition, co-ed event, it does not follow UCI rules. You are racing for points, and you are allowed to gain a lap if you can. Each rider must ride two laps, then exchange. Each rider must ride five sprints unless there's a crash or a mechanical problem. The rider who's out is to rejoin the race as soon as possible through an exchange. Referees will pull riders who are off the back. You are expected to know the rules."

Rosie looked around, for riders who were not paying attention or who hadn't yet gotten to the start line. They shouldn't need much information now, just enough to help them focus. They knew this official well. She was from the Houston track, known as Alkek velodrome and one of the most experienced officials in the U.S. Riders showed the appropriate level of respect for her advisories, waiting patiently. When she was convinced that riders were sufficiently focused and ready —

"Riders ready..." counseled the Madame Official -- and the whistle...

Half of each team rolled out for the first lap while the other half waited on the rail for the expected start pistol once they came around and showed they were all together. 40 exchanges, which could be as minimal as touching, would be tiring, but rests would be good. Challenging!

The Plan

Chilly listened to the instructions, reminding himself of differences from the official Madisons he had ridden. He had a few minutes to breathe deep and try, as much as was possible, to relax. He was pretty good at relaxing while keyed up for a race. It was sort of a requirement. You couldn't succumb to nerves, you had to fight them all the time, since they become more hinderance than help if you couldn't get them under control. There had been days when he just "lost it" and realized in the race that followed that it was just energy down the drain.

He never had a good race unless he could gather himself together and get in that "other place" right before a race.

He breathed and relaxed, replaying the 2016 World Madison event in his mind for his own personal WIN! He didn't know who Rosie thought she was, but he was definitely "Cav" today -- Mark Cavendish of the United Kingdom, road sprinter superb, with over 100 professional wins, many with an electrifying finish on and off the track. He hoped Rosie was channeling Bradley Wiggins, unbeatable on both road and track, winning so many races and venues that readers went dizzy trying to keep them all straight. He had won the World Madison three times (twice with Cav) and held the World Hour record. The 2016 Madison was one of the greatest races he had ever seen. And now, Chilly/Cav would repeat that performance with his partner Rosie/Wiggo. He imagined that, happily. Recalling Cav's crash, he promised himself that if he went down, he'd do exactly what Cav did — WIN ANYWAY!

Rosie pushed off with the others, quickly finding her place in the pack, riding peacefully for the moment. Rosie could see some were nervous, but the Grand Prix was a quality race, and didn't attract many novices. Most "real" Madison riders had practiced and raced the event many times before, first and foremost, the "handsling", the single most important element of a Madison to understand -- and to be able to do! She saw Sheryl, but she didn't bring any attention to herself...

Mike, watching the race surrounded by his "brothers", was ready for the starting pistol this time. All of them were together on the backstretch, watching his girl Rosie and Moocher's boy Chilly. Old memories of war would not interrupt his oldest memory of that glorious Great Day in Bloomington when he saved the day by filling in after Dave's crash. He was mentally back in time, before all the trauma, all the death, and all the brain damaging noise. Life was good, as good as it could ever get. Right now.

A man Moocher recognized as Andy's dad from Indy walked by. "Hey, how you all doing today?" He said idly, as he kept walking.

"Well, we're a little disturbed by the developments in the Middle East, but otherwise we're good." responded Cyril.

Moocher chuckled. That Cyril. What a joker. Dave and Mike hadn't heard either one of them. Their eyes were locked on the start of the race. Riders gathered together on this first lap, knowing that if they were not together in turn four, the gun wouldn't go off. They would have to ride around a whole 'nother lap until they were all together.

But, they all did what they needed to do. As they came around turn three, Rosie felt the pack dig in a little, anticipating the start. Coming around turn four, they almost stalled to show the officials they were all together. It was good. Then the gun went off! And the pace picked up rapidly.

Rosie knew that strong riders would be in the race. The new "up-and-comers" were always wild cards, especially at a track known for an excellent training program like Baker. The Marymoor track offered a top program since the 1970's, shepherded by the famous Jerry Baker, after whom the track was now named. Baker always believed in programs for even the youngest riders. If they could keep their bikes upright, Baker found a race for them, from the pedal bikes to the push bikes, to those with training wheels.

The "Kiddie Kilo" on the velodrome was famous to bike fan parents of the smallest kids who loved bicycle racing. Baker loved watching "his children" experience the joy of "competition" and grow up to be competitors. He knew that predicting performance was not possible, but starting kids on the track was fun! Baker was gone now. Rosie wished she could have met him.

Rosie felt a nudge on her right. Her attention suddenly reverted to those around her, riding easy, not yet ready to pick up the pace. She tried to "read" the others to see who could stand their ground and who might be intimidated in a pack. She recognized one rider, an occasional visitor to the San Diego track. She seemed to be experienced and comfortable in the crowd, Rosie wouldn't need to worry about her. They came around on the first lap, all still pretty well together, a little strung out, but no one in any hurry on this big track. It was only the first lap...

Suddenly, a rider she'd never seen before shot out of the pack, diving down the banking, leaving the pack behind. Another rider chased, then another. Rosie watched Sheryl and the speed of the riders who took off, trying to decide whether to join them or focus on Sheryl. She decided to stay with Sheryl. Chilly told her Andy's was the team to beat, though Rosie knew there would be others. For now, she'd wait. The pace of the pack picked up, but only to reel in the riders off the front.

The "off-the-front" riders managed to put a gap between themselves and the pack, but they weren't able to stay away. The exchanges began. Rosie looked for Chilly and saw him riding slowly at the top of the banking. He was watching for her and accelerated at her approach. He dove down the track to match her speed, grabbed her hand cautiously and she threw him forward. He looked for Andy, but knew it was too early to worry about him. For now they just needed to ride straight, stay up, and hope all the other riders knew what they were doing. Riders were cautious and getting a feel for others on the track.

The next set of laps were covered before Chilly even knew it. This race was getting FAST! He looked for Rosie. She was "up track" and ready. Her throw had been good. He didn't want his to be too soft, but he didn't want to startle her, either. There were 15 other teams on the track, and he only knew three of them. He grabbed Rosie's hand and propelled her forward steadily. He felt her readiness and her smooth transition. This would work.

"THROW ME!" she yelled after him, maintaining her speed and digging down, accelerating after riders in front of her. Sheryl was ahead of her right now. Andy had thrown Sheryl too hard and she was just recovering while Andy pulled up track, yelling after her, issuing orders. Rosie felt sorry for her. She rode up behind her, settling on her wheel. Once Sheryl recovered from the exchange, Rosie knew why Andy had picked her for his partner. She was fast! While Rosie had no problem riding her wheel, she also realized that they were passing other riders somewhat casually. She might have been a little rocky in the exchange,

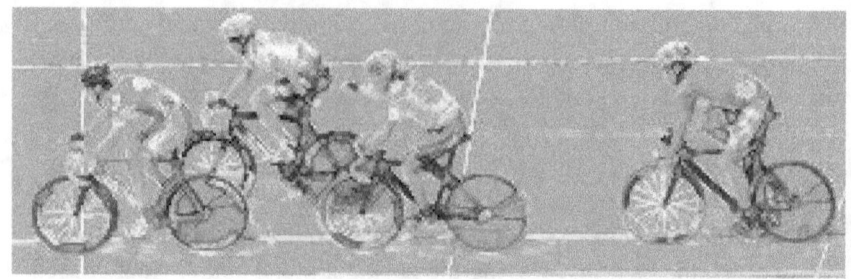

but this woman Sheryl was a good wheel to ride. Rosie sat on for a half a lap, then moved to pass her. Sheryl gave no resistance and just settled on Rosie's wheel.

That's okay, Rosie thought, I'm okay trading off -- for now. Sheryl seemed to agree. Rosie didn't know if Sheryl knew of Chilly's rivalry with Andy. Surely she wouldn't be so congenial if she did. On the other hand it occurred to her that Sheryl and she might be great Team Pursuit or Team Sprint partners at some future National Championship. She obviously knew how to trade leads "Team Pursuit style".

Rosie's Madison Sprint

Rosie heard the bell signifying the sprint, throwing everyone into a higher level of excitement. Rosie suddenly realized that a rider was coming up on her right and it wasn't Sheryl. The jersey said it was a TeamSEA rider, who was probably way more used to the Baker track than either Rosie or Sheryl. The Seattle rider pulled ahead, followed by Sheryl, who had been on her wheel. Rosie didn't care about the Seattle rider, Team SEA was welcome to the 5 points if she could hold her lead. Rosie wanted the points Sheryl would get if she crossed the finish line before her. Rosie was holding Sheryl off as both chased the Seattle rider, but the finish was coming fast, and she realized that they might both be "throwing" their bikes for those three points. When they crossed the finish line together, Rosie threw her bike as far as she could while sneaking a peek to try to see whether she or Sheryl crossed first. She knew she wasn't supposed to look, but she really wanted to know right away. She couldn't tell, it was so close.

They'd have to wait for the verdict, but Rosie was optimistic. She'd practiced throwing her bike a million times when Eddie B had been at the track and told her how important it was to learn. He had made her do it over and over and over... and she had gotten good at it -- especially when Shaun had made her do it a couple hundred more times after Eddie. Both said it was a matter of timing, which could be taught and learned. She wasn't sure of how important it was until she watched a lot of "bike throw" videos, she learned that it didn't matter where her body was, it was the position of the bike that mattered. Unless the front of her wheel crossed before the other rider, even the smallest bit, she would would get less points.

She cursed herself when she heard the announcement that Sheryl had managed to get her wheel across a tiny bit farther than Rosie. Sheryl had gotten the coveted 3 points for the first sprint. Well, that's okay, better the 3 than the 5 points that the Seattle rider got. Rosie got 2. She'd better watch that Seattle rider. She shouldn't have been surprised because some of the best riders in the country came from the Seattle track.

But she couldn't think about any of that now.

On the next set of laps, Rosie was sure that Chilly would be ready to take the next sprint. She hoped he hadn't been mad at her "loss" on the last one. That's okay, it was a long race and there were more sprints coming up. Rosie felt herself warmed up now, ready for the next exchange, knowing that it would not be long. She looked for Chilly up-track, coming around with her hand on her hip, maintaining her speed. No light-weight stuff, she needed him to know that she could <u>throw</u> so he'd do the same and she could accelerate even faster! As soon as she felt his hand, she grabbed it, turned slightly, then pulled him forward. They were both moving very fast, but the pack was strung out. Rosie moved up track, to ride slow, and await the next exchange.

Chilly planned to make up those points on his next sprint. He was again surprised at her power and her coordination. The throw she did this time was stronger than anything in practice or before. She knew that they'd need to finish better in sprints in order to win. Competition probably brought out her competitive side like it did his. Some riders blew up, some grew stronger. Apparently Rosie was the latter. He wouldn't underestimate her again. Their practice paid off. They were a good team.

On the next set of laps, TeamDyMinn (Andy and Sheryl) and TeamSEA maintained their pace, Chilly following closely. It was unlikely anyone would slow from now on. This would be a long, hard race. Rosie knew that the tiny bit she had slowed when she tried to look at Sheryl's finish had probably won it for Sheryl. She would not make that mistake again. Rosie, you <u>know</u> what to do! she scolded herself.

Chilly was obviously a good pack rider, as Rosie watched him over the next set of laps. He'd always find a good wheel. Danger accelerated as the next sprint approached. Everyone sprinted as the pack strung out at speed. There were three other riders around Chilly, one of them Andy. A rider Chilly didn't know came down track, almost dumping him. Chilly yelled at him, but it slowed his momentum at a crucial point in the sprint. Andy was ahead of that rider, winning the sprint, while the best Chilly could manage was second, again giving them only 3 points to Andy's 5. They'd need to do better than that!

Exchanges settled into a succession of tense moments interspersed with laps full of speed and riding wheels, but the Madison was a race where everyone knew that one false move at high speeds could result in a crash, and the riders were acutely aware that co-ed was strange for some of them, but by-and-large, they were careful of the added danger from unexpected teams. All things considered, it went pretty well. Besides, they wanted to race, not get hauled off in an ambulance. They could see the EMT crews sitting by the side of the track.

The bell rang, signifying the beginning of another sprint. Now it was Rosie's turn to take points. She took off, suddenly realizing that Sheryl was on her wheel, and this time she had no intention on trading pulls. Instead, Sheryl planned to sit in Rosie's draft for an easier ride, then come around to beat her at the line. Damn wheel-sucker. They passed several riders, but Rosie could not shake Sheryl. Suddenly, Sheryl seemed to decelerate. She left Sheryl to contest the sprint with the TeamSEA rider and finished ahead. Hooray! She had managed to gain 5 points, in oxygen debt.

She didn't fully understand why Sheryl seemed to slow before that sprint, allowing two riders to pass her and only taking one point. She didn't look tired. That was odd. Gasping, Rosie pulled out of the sprinter's lane looking for Chilly.

Out of the corner of her eye, she saw Sheryl push into a semi-sprint, leaving everyone else behind as they slowed, looking for their partners. She continued her sprint to the far side, where Andy waited. "What is she doing?" Rosie asked within herself. Sheryl had "rested" on her wheel for a lap and a half, so she was not as tired as Rosie at that point. At first, Rosie thought she was confused, but as she continued to watch and look for Chilly, she realized the real reason for Sheryl's push -- she and Andy planned to take a lap and she was giving Andy the biggest lead she could.

This was a risky move on any track because a team could blow up trying to do what couldn't easily be done -- gain a lap on the field -- especially on a big track like Baker. It was hard on a 250 meter track, as the Worlds fans saw in the 2016 Worlds, but on a 400 meter track, it was flirting with competitive death. Many riders on Rosie's home track of 333 meters had a tough time maintaining enough speed to do it, but Rosie had not even thought that Sheryl and Andy would try to do it on this big track. Sheryl kept sprinting, creating a gap from the pack for Andy to pick up. Chilly saw it too, but Rosie had not come around yet to handsling him in. She hadn't anticipated Sheryl's move. He hoped for a BIG throw from Rosie so he could catch Andy. Chilly sprinted down track to meet her.

"They're trying to steal a lap!" he yelled.

"I know, GO, GO" she yelled back.

The Seattle audience was well educated on race dynamics and could see what was happening. Andy had no intention of staying with the pack. If his team could ride off the front and circle the track, rejoining the pack at the back, they would be a "lap up". In other words, if everyone else had ridden 32 laps, he would be considered to have ridden 33, and now would be "the winner" on every lap after, whether he got points or not. Other riders could still contest for points, but they'd all be one lap down. ANY team that is a "lap up", automatically wins the race, no matter what points anyone has -- that part was consistent with UCI rules. If Andy's team even had only 5 point to Chilly's 35 points, Andy would still be named the winner. If they were both a "lap up" the riders with the most points wins.

Chilly was sure he could "reel" Andy in, so he accelerated immediately, helped by Rosie's throw to get up to speed. He was gaining, but then, what they had all tried to avoid happened -- a crash, on the home stretch.

Chilly was just coming out of turn four, chasing Andy, who was heading toward turn one. Chilly planned to catch him by the backstretch. All of a sudden, that sound of a crash that every rider recognizes, forced him to instinctively swing wide, slowing to escape it. Another rider wasn't so lucky. A sloppy exchange plus overlapped wheels caused three people to go down.

Chilly knew what the officials would do. They would declare the race "neutral", meaning "hold your positions" until any injured riders were taken care of. It didn't look like a bad crash, just one that would hold them up until all riders and bikes were out of the way of charging riders. Chilly was now on the home stretch, in front of the whole crowd. He immediately checked to see who went down. It was a team that had made him nervous when he watched them do a couple of exchanges earlier. They looked like they were being careful, but in an environment of raw speed like the Madison could be anything could happen. Was anyone actually hurt or did they just needed a short break to get back on their bikes and reenter the race? This would take a little time. Meanwhile riders were supposed to maintain their positions.

Chilly watched the EMT's jump into action as the riders with the pack slowed to maintain their places. The trouble is, all riders did not maintain their places. While everyone watched the EMT's and officials, Chilly kept his eyes on Andy, who had not slowed his pace until he came up to an official who signaled him to slow. Then Chilly watched Andy put on a big show. Oh sure, he hadn't realized his mistake! He didn't know! Sure.

In fact, Andy had moved another quarter lap ahead of Chilly, who had slowed because of the crash, as well as the neutral lap he knew was coming. It appeared the officials were too busy making sure no one was hurt to bother watching Andy closely.

Chilly could lodge a protest after the race about Andy's behavior, which might be honored, but only if the officials thought that the error made a difference in the final outcome. If they decided it would not have changed the final result, they would not likely issue any sort of penalty. It was a long shot imagining that IF Andy won, Chilly might be the "default" winner due to a protest -- and that only if he was second. Too many variables made that scenario too hard to predict. Chilly knew that if he intended to win, he would also need to gain the lap he now realized that Andy/Team DyMinn would probably now be able to gain -- thanks to the crash and officials' concern with downed riders. By the time riders were cleaned up and back on their bikes, Chilly could see that Andy had managed to stretch a quarter lap lead to more like a two-thirds lap lead. Chilly wasn't sure he could make up that much of a difference before the next exchange -- but he would have to try.

As Chilly suspected, by the time Andy did the next exchange with Sheryl, she was able to maintain and extend enough of a lead to "bridge the gap" and catch up to the back of the pack. Andy's team was now up one lap, giving him a clear win, regardless of any points Chilly and Rosie had. Chilly found himself barely beating the Seattle riders, who were excellent at all skills, exchange, sprint, and bike throw. Chilly began to see the TeamSEA riders as a challenge he had not anticipated, though he should have known. Retired National and World Champions coached at Baker. At least the TeamSEA guy had held his place and not been sneaky like Andy.

Coming around on the next lap, Chilly found Rosie and completed a textbook exchange.

Early in the next set, before the fifth sprint, a young female rider went off the front of the pack. She was unknown and from the Kissena track in New York, an old track with many good riders over the years, but no one knew this team. The young girl kept riding strong, but the pack let her go, believing that she'd fade. Lots of riders ride off the front, either for attention or in idle hopes, but few actually made the distance

around, even on a smaller track. The Kissena riders had shown themselves to be no challenge so far in the race, huddling in the pack, though Kissea had managed to get some points. Riders watching from within the pack didn't believe they were strong enough to gain a lap. They fully expected them to fade. The bell was still several laps away, and instead of expending needless energy chasing a non-threatening team, they felt it a better idea to just rest up for that sprint. Meanwhile, the young Kissena riders slowly and steadily extended their lead.

What riders in the pack didn't think about was that the Kissena track was also a big track, even bigger than Baker, so the Kissena riders knew well the demands of a big track. They often traveled to Trexlertown, the Holy Grail of tracks, to compete, so they were experienced.

"They'll slow," riders in the pack kept saying to each other, "don't bother to chase, we'll pull them back".

As it came closer to the bell signaling the sprint, Kissena had a big lead and several other riders began to chase, including TeamIcyRose, partly just to contest the sprint, leaving some in the pack behind. The Kissena riders pushed harder, fading somewhat, but still maintaining their gap ahead of the pack. It looked like Kissena might actually manage to gain a lap, not because they were so fast, but because they were strong and partly just because the pack didn't chase. As the pack strung out with increased speed on the front, some of the riders farther back were fading, allowing Kissena to gain on them more rapidly, even though she hadn't increased her speed. Rosie recalled the young Kissena girl from the

Pursuit rounds. She did well in that race, everyone thinking that was just a fluke, too. Third place, Rosie recalled, but since no one knew her, they sort of ignored her. They wouldn't make that mistake again.

Now Kissena, a team no one expected to do anything significant, did another quick exchange and, with a new rider and a gap, the guy who rode for Kissena easily closed the gap to the back of the pack. Now Kissena was up a lap and had a total of 6 points. They were in second place!

The two teams who were a "lap up", had first and second places locked up --unless IcyRose or other teams could manage to gain a lap too. After five sprints, Chilly and Rosie just tried to ride the race and maintain their positions. It was such a fast race, everyone was getting tired. Team IcyRose had managed to gain quite a few points, but they were aware that, by this time, points didn't matter.

The points standings: Team DyMinn (Andy and Sheryl) - 14 points -- plus, one lap up; Kissena - 12 points plus one lap up; Team IcyRose (Chilly and Rosie) - 15 points; Team SEA - 16. A couple of other teams had managed to gain a point or two, but nothing meant anyone was going to win except those who were one lap up.

Chilly and Rosie were not the only team realizing this. This would be one of the hardest races either had ever contested. At least they both had confidence in their partnership.

The Watchers

Dave and Moocher were stomping around, worried. All four brothers were yelling themselves hoarse every time Chilly or Rosie came around. Mike was thrilled because his girl was on the team with the most points!

"What are you worried about, they're winning!" crowed Mike.

Everyone had been so busy yelling, no one had stopped to explain the race to Mike and Cyril. As usual, Cyril was just happy to be part of things. He admired athletes. He had worked on visualization and other techniques with several of them at the University. He was not into winning as much as optimal performance and health. The wives had decided to sit on the other side, closer to the announcer and the finish line. Nancy and Joelle could explain rule details to the other ladies. Joelle would be able to describe the great track racing in Europe, in London, Paris, Milan and Amsterdam, among others. There was so many tracks in Europe that most bicycling enthusiasts over there knew rules quite well, but in the U.S., unless fans were lucky enough to have a track close by, this kind of racing was almost unknown.

Meanwhile, as Dave and Moocher stomped and lamented, Mike got irritated.

"Look you guys," he insisted, "They have more points than anyone else. They look really good together. Don't worry, they'll get more points and win. Really! Watch! They're winning! What a team!"

Dave and Moocher looked at each other.

"You go ahead and explain it." Moocher said, and he sat down.

"You don't understand, Mike," said Dave. "There are two teams who have gained a lap. Those teams are a lap up. That means that no matter what happens, no matter how many points any other team has, they will be the only ones who will be declared the winners. Then the points will decide who gets the places after them. But it's laps first, then points. Rosie's team could have 100 points and the other team 5 points, but the team that is "up a lap" (a lap ahead) will beat her."

"What?" objected Mike. "She has way more points, how can she be behind anyone else?"

"Those are the rules, Mike. It makes no difference about anything else, Laps first, then points. Period. Those are Madison rules."

"That SUCKS!" Mike yelled, stomping his feet. Other parents and fans looked over. Mike was a little embarrassed, but still fumed. "That's not what happened in that other race!"

"The other race was a Points race," Dave explained. "In the Madison race it's laps, <u>then</u> points."

"Do they know that?" asked Mike, wondering why they hadn't ridden harder to make that gain in laps.

"Yes, don't worry, the both know it, but this is a big track and it's very hard to gain a lap here. It's a long way and riders to go off the front trying to take a lap are more often chased down or they get tired, so it's a big deal to try to do that here. What they don't want to do is blow their whole race, exhaust themselves so much that they "blow up" and lose the race worse than if they hadn't put out all that effort. Right now they're in third. They don't want to blow it so they get nothing." Dave explained, patiently.

Mike was quiet for a few minutes, trying to digest the injustice of his little girl having more points but still not being in first place.

"Well they'll just have to get that lap!" he blurted out loudly, suddenly. He walked to the rail as Rosie came abound.

"You're down a lap, Rosie!" yelled Mike. He waited until the next time she came around.

"Come on, Rosie, get that lap!" yelled Mike again.

Dave and Moocher knew that riders often had a plan or could only do certain things within certain conditions, so they didn't yell at Rosie or Chilly to pick up that needed extra lap. Cyril understood in theory, but couldn't think of any cheers that he thought would help. Mike, though, was used to military discipline. If your superior officer ordered you to "Take that ridge!" you didn't question it. There was a job to do, a goal to be achieved. You set your mind on the goal and you DID it. That's what he expected of Rosie. Take that "ridge"! Accomplish the goal! Second best (or third) was not good enough.

Rosie knew her dad thought like that, but he had long ago given up getting mad when expecting that which she could not do. Since she was very little he realized that she would try as hard as she could in everything she tried to do. However, she would also try extra hard to make him proud at this race, so she looked even harder for some way to do what she needed to do to win. They had three more sprints. Maybe they could manage to gain a lap in one of those sprints. It would be very challenging, but she knew that Chilly was "in", so to speak. Whether he led or she led, they were both prepared to give it their all in a massive attempt, even if they lost the race and didn't even get a place, at this point. It was a matter of giving what they had.

At the exchange after the sixth sprint, Chilly shouted "Ready? LAP!"

Rosie knew that he meant. "Yes!" she called back.

This time it was Rosie's turn to take off at the end of the sprint, planning to leave the pack as soon as possible after the exchange. She came around with a good lead and he grabbed her hand and she threw him, her hardest throw so far. He took off to extend her lead if he could. He noticed she had been on the wheel of the TeamSEA woman. He popped onto wheel of the Team SEA guy, Jim, who was also getting a big lead from his partner. Both knew that to survive and be in the money, they were going to have to gain a lap. They went into Pursuit mode on a joint mission, alternating leads and drafts.

Unfortunately for Rosie, the other teams had already been through several sprints with her and now viewed her as a threat. In the next set, Sheryl chased and jumped on her wheel, along with the Seattle rider and another unknown rider. The unknown rider was dropped first. That left Sheryl and Seattle on Rosie's wheel. Sheryl hesitated when she put her head down and almost collided with another rider in front of them. Rosie and Seattle did not slow down, dropping Sheryl. "Sorry, Sheryl," Rosie thought, "but I have a job to do..." and she pushed even harder to make sure Sheryl was left behind. She heard her yelling at the unfortunate rider who had gotten in her way. Seattle and Rosie pushed decisively until Sheryl was a quarter of a lap down. Seattle was obviously very experienced. She knew how to pull through so transitions were smooth, and how to anticipate others' lines and ride around others, especially the ones struggling with the race itself. Everyone was getting tired. Rosie just hoped they stayed alert. She certainly was.

When it came to the next exchange, Teams IcyRose and SEA were about one-third of a lap ahead. They searched for their partners.

Since both men were experienced Madison riders, they had been watching and were ready to charge down track and continue the chase after the back of the pack so they, too, could be a lap up.

Rosie got there first. Chilly charged down the track and she gave him a massive push. The Seattle riders exchanged with the same powerful momentum. They had an identical plan -- take a lap so they could be judged on points. TeamSEA planned to at least be in third, IF they could make up the lap. To be fourth and not in the money at all, was unacceptable. They had to make up a lap.

It became like a double team race. Both knew what they had to do. They had to exchange together, not knock anyone else down, and not get knocked down themselves. It felt smooth, like they had practiced together, just as though they had already practiced this two-team Madison. Even so, they had a LONG way to go. The Kissena team did NOT want anyone else to make up that lap, because, according to points, that would make them fourth. They wanted to continue at second. Andy wanted to compete against a rider he figured only gained a lap because people underestimated him. He assumed he'd be able to hold a rider like that off in the sprint, no problem.

Kissena picked up the pace. If they could keep up the speed and the pack would follow, they MIGHT be able to fatigue IcyRose enough with each exchange that they wouldn't be able to close the gap to the back of the main pack. Team DyMinn rested in the pack, but tried to keep the momentum going strong to burn out IcyRose and TeamSEA. The chasers (SEA and IcyRose) went around several times, struggling with the distance, but as they maintained their beautiful "team pursuit of two" negotiating exchanges smoothly. Some parts of the pack became more fatigued. DyMinn and Kissena could maintain speed and distance in the front, but they could not hurry up those in the back who were still considered part of "the pack", but fading. Two other teams had tried to follow IcyRose and SEA, but they had faded. Riders in the back came closer and closer to enabling Teams IcyRose and SEA to gain that lap.

If the sprint came up and SEA and/or IcyRose had still not joined the pack, they'd get 5 points for being off the front, but once they joined the back of the pack, both be up a lap. They could get points if they could get to the front before the next bell, but that was not as big a problem. They had to get that lap or points would not matter. They kept pushing. By this time, Team DyMinn were fighting to stay in front to defend their lead. They would need more points, if they were going to lock in a win.

As Rosie came around, reaching for Chilly, Andy threw Sheryl in a sloppy exchange that sent her wobbling into Chilly. Andy charged forward as Chilly went down, blindsided and unable to recover.

"Sorry!" he heard Andy yell as he went past. He wasn't sure who Andy was talking to. He knew that Andy was sorry, not because of causing Chilly to go down, but because he was embarrassed at his bad throw and Sheryl's subsequent wobbling into Chilly. He was probably calling to Sheryl, since he knew it was his fault more than hers. He certainly didn't mean to crash his own team member but he was fine with Chilly going down.

Rosie realized immediately that, since she and Chilly had not made contact with each other, they could not be considered to have made a valid exchange, which was mandatory unless there was a crash. But as soon as she heard the crash, she knew that her job was to sprint! While that was usually a reaction to another team's crashing, she instinctively sprinted toward the closest wheel in front of her, barely aware that it was Team SEA's. Jim had turned to see who crashed, slowing slightly, but once he saw it was Chilly, he went back to his race. He continued

chasing the pack, and didn't even notice Rosie. He was getting there, but had to push to maintain enough speed to reach them.

Now Chilly was really mad. He was off the track, just on the infield, so he knew it wouldn't be necessary to call for a "neutral race". He rested for a millisecond, just to feel whether anything was broken. He knew adrenaline could mask injury. His body did not tell him anything was broken or severely injured, so he looked down, trying to get out of his pedals making sure he was out of the way of other riders. He had tight clips, plus double straps holding his feet in his pedals, so there was a lot to undo. He stood up as officials and the EMT crew quickly ascertained his injuries -- or lack of them. He tried to push them aside so he could jump back on the track, but they refused to allow him to rejoin the race until they felt he could continue without injury to himself or other riders. Rosie would have to ride at least one of his laps, but what would happen to their lead? Two more sprints and the race would be over. He doubted that Rosie could keep up with a group of charging male riders. Maybe she could find a wheel. Was there still any hope of them gaining a lap?

He searched for her in the pack. He couldn't see her, which was worrisome. Had she dropped out? That would end the race for them.

Suddenly he noticed where the Seattle rider was, approaching the back of the pack. He looked for Rosie and found her: she was on his wheel! He'd have to get back on the track and exchange NOW if they were doing to complete their exchange so Chilly could resume the race — and maybe get back on Team Sea's wheel.

Good girl, Rosie! He screamed to himself in excitement. They still had a chance. He grabbed his bike, checked it quickly, then hopped on. The official who cleared him to reenter the race held him so that he could to re-clip into his pedals. Then picked up speed, cutting through the other riders to get to the top of the track and wait for Rosie. He hoped that their teamwork had extended to her realizing that he would try again to exchange with her on the next lap. His adrenaline was so high, he knew he could close the distance and sprint to the front again.

Rosie felt strong on Jim's wheel. He was aware of what had happened, though he had wondered for a minute what a woman was doing on his wheel in the "guy's" segment of the race. He figured she was the teammate of the crashed rider. He was a big guy, and she fit compactly into his draft. He was a strong rider, one of the strongest on the track. He didn't mind Rosie sucking his wheel, though it would have been great to have someone to trade off with. He knew she couldn't pull and hoped Chilly was okay, partly just to help him gain the lap he was fighting for if he could get back into the race.

Rosie could probably make it for one more lap, but not for two more after that. If they exchanged so that she was back with the women, another woman would not provide that same big slipstream as Jim so she could both ride fast and rest. Then she and Chilly would have no hope of completing that extra lap gain. She hoped that Chilly was okay, but felt a little guilt at her first instinct wishing him good health for their race, then for him in general. Even if she could manage to finish the race by riding other riders' wheels, she could never make that lap gain without him.

She approached the area of their last exchange, seeing Chilly on his bike, waiting for her. She extending her hand and pushed Chilly forward with all her might. He almost crashed into Jim, but fortunately, Jim didn't realize it and Chilly recovered quickly.

A short time later, she saw Andy coming up, trying in vain to stretch the pack out to stop the lap gain, but still too far back to be effective, plus, leading the pack behind didn't help defeat the lap gain attempt if the pack kept up enough not to be pulled. He saw what a great throw Rosie had done in spite of her fatigue and that it had allowed Chilly to rejoin Jim. He wished Sheryl could throw that well. He wished Chilly had crashed again. He decided to rag on Rosie, maybe rattle her.

"Hey!" cried Andy, swerving to avoid the contact. "Stupid girl, don't you know how to throw?" he screamed.

In fact, she did know how to throw and her intent was to throw Chilly hard enough to help him get back up to speed on TeamSEA's wheel, which he did. Too bad, Andy, she thought.

"Good girl!" thought Chilly. "I picked a good one!"

Stupid girl? thought Rosie at Andy's remark. She knew why Andy was trying to insult her, so it just made her proud. She felt sorry that Sheryl had probably endured far worse verbal assaults.

As Rosie threw Chilly in their next exchange, TeamSEA had anticipated a change of pace and took off. He didn't have too much more distance to rejoining the pack, but he was also getting tired. He needed help, not for someone to just sit on his his wheel. But Chilly didn't hesitate, he knew that Jim would be getting tired and he jumped on his wheel, so mad, he was barely on Jim's wheel for a minute, when he

decided he come around for a much stronger pull. Pretty soon Rosie would have to take over again. He hoped she could do it, but he at least wanted to give her as long a lead as he could. It appeared Jim was up to it. He settled on Chilly's wheel for a strong pull.

When he came around this time, Chilly could see that Rosie was waiting anxiously. He wasn't sure how hard to throw her, but decided that it was now or never and threw her hard. She answered his throw with a surge that caused TeamSEA to struggle to catch her. Chilly was surprised, but thrilled that she seemed to have recovered so quickly. As the women off the front fought for the sprint win, those at the back faded further from exhaustion.

With the speed picking up and more riders fading on the back (but not far enough to be pulled), Teams IcyRose and SEA saw their goals come closer and closer as they maintained their pace, trading pulls. Finally, as the crowd roared its approval, they closed the gap.

Rosie (IcyRose and TeamSEA) did it!! Her dad hardly had any voice left, he'd been screaming so hard.

Now it was all about points — for these teams, anyway. Standings, going into the last set of laps before the sprint: TeamIcyRose: 17. TeamDyMinn: 18. TeamSEA: 16, and Kissena: 14. It was VERY close and all set for an upset. Who would get those strategic 5 points? Who would get the 3-2-1 behind? Someone might not be in the money. The winner would be decided in the final sprint.

The next exchange was good. All riders had recovered as much as they could when riding an 80 lap race at top speeds while moving in and out around other riders of varying abilities. It was getting very close now, very close. One more sprint. The next exchange plus two remaining laps would decide the race. All riders wanted to set their team member up for the best place possible.

Rosie put on her final burst of speed with everything she had. She was near the front and passed other riders to find Sheryl's wheel. She recognized that there were other riders to worry about, including TeamSEA and Kissena, but she knew Chilly was most concerned with Andy, so she focused on Sheryl, who pushed even harder in an effort to drop her. "No way!" thought Rosie, summoning anger and maintaining her position in the draft.

Andy didn't like seeing Sheryl and Rosie so close to each other. He wanted Sheryl to drop Rosie and give him a lead on Chilly, but he would still have two laps to cover before the finish line. He was sure he could take Chilly in the sprint. He'd seen him crash and knew that he might be affected by the injuries -- maybe. He swung down for the exchange with Sheryl. Chilly charged after him, connecting with Rosie who threw him with every once of her remaining strength. He and Andy were now neck-and-neck. Andy tried to drop Chilly in the two laps before the finish, but could not. He felt somewhat surprised, but figured the final sprint would sort it out. He wasn't too worried. He could beat this rube. He was more worried about Jim, the TeamSEA rider who was right behind them. He knew Jim had a sprint. The Kissena rider was on Jim's wheel.

Chilly slowed slightly as Andy pushed forward to try to shake him, but Chilly settled back on Andy's wheel, much to Andy's distress. He knew that Chilly planned to be there on the last lap, "slingshotting" out of turn 4 and winning the race at the last minute at the line. That was exactly what Andy had planned, too, but it wouldn't work unless he had someone to slingshot around! They couldn't slow too much or riders behind, who also intended on winning, knew this was it, this was the final sprint.

Andy tried to leave Chilly behind repeatedly, but Chilly wouldn't budge. Andy stood up on the backstretch to sprint, trying a jump so sudden that Chilly would be dropped. That worked for an instant, but then Chilly was back on his wheel. It was like he had a bungie cord attached to Andy's wheel. They were coming to turn four, furiously sprinting, bikes and lines unstable from the effort. As Chilly began to come around, slingshotting out of turn four as expected, Andy swung

wide, pushing Chilly up track, making contact, which was against the rules, but might only be ruled as a violation if officials saw it as changing the outcome of the race.

It only made Chilly angrier, a big mistake, as Chilly charged on. With other riders sprinting behind them, Andy and Chilly were locked into a struggle that would end in seconds, both riders watching the finish line accelerate toward them. They knew that throwing their bikes was the only way to win — if they could!

As the finish line barreled at them, Chilly harnessed all speed he had, angrily disciplining himself for the finish. DON'T think of Andy now. Give everything you've got. Don't look. Put your head down and, at the finish, throw your bike at the finish as far as you possibly can! There is nothing else. The crowd SCREAMED its excitement.

Chilly had no idea who won. He did a "textbook" throw at full speed and left the win up to the Forces of the Universe.

He and Andy pulled up track, heaving, out of the way of other riders who were also charging for the finish. They didn't look at each other, then Chilly extended his hand in good will. While he almost didn't answer, Andy put out his hand for the briefest handshake. One of them won, and it was too late now to continue the fight. Neither lost easily, but both knew what good sportsmanship looked like, and Andy didn't want to snub a rider he might have beaten. That wouldn't look good to the crowd.

The crowd was going wild with excitement, not only for that contest, but also for other teams in back of Chilly and Andy. Seattle, Kissena and another rider were locked in another furious battle. The third rider could only place fifth, if at all. Seattle was in the middle, buffeted by riders on both sides. Lucky he was a good bike handler, or the whole group might have gone down. He pulled ahead, partly to disengage from the others. He won by a wheel length. The other two riders finished just behind, all pulling up track. They came in exhausted, giving what little they had left. All were exhausted and happy the race was over.

The announcer offered no judgment as to the winner.

"We'll have to wait for the officials to decide the winner of that race." as he offered names of riders and teams who came after.

Chilly heard him as he rode toward the warm-up circle. He would feel tense until the final decision, win or lose. He saw Rosie warming down.

"That was great, Rosie, good save! I don't know how I clipped that wheel."

"Are you okay?" she asked "She was out of control."

"I wasn't sure for a minute or two, you know how it is, but nothing that a little silvadene won't fix." he joked, referring to a commonly used protector for skin injury.

"My dad has some great stuff they use in the military he can give you some of that, too if you want." she offered as she looked at the road rash on his leg and at his ripped jersey.

"I knew there was some reason I shaved my legs. Easier to clean up!" Chilly exalted. "Besides showing off my legs." they both chuckled.

Chilly looked back at the announcer's stand, where officials were gathered. "I wish they'd figure that out." he remarked, as he rode, somewhat "buzzed" from his effort. "I'm glad that's over!"

"Me too!" Rosie responded.

They rode a few more times around the warm-up track. Andy and Sheryl riding around slowly too, but no one was talking to each other except to congratulate on a race well-rode. "Good race" they each said to each other, then went back to silence.

They just waited.

Finally, the announcer came back on.

"In one of the closest finishes we've ever seen on this track, with about a 5 millimeter lead, the winner of this year's Baker Grand Prix is the team of IcyRose, from San Diego and Indy, pull out a win! Congratulations, Team IcyRose!"

Chilly jumped off his bike and pulled Rosie off of hers as another team member ran over and held it up.

"We did it!" he yelled for anyone listening. "We did it!" Jumping up and down together.

Andy looked challenging at the announcer's stand, but he knew that the time it took to come to a decision made the results very unlikely to be challenged. Officials wanted fairness and a good race. No one would look at a photo finish result and try to say it was different. He might be able to lodge a protest, but what would it be? He couldn't think of one that would stick. Chilly had won, fair and square. He walked over to shake hands.

"Okay, Chilly, you took that one, fine, but I don't know how." he said.

Chilly didn't answer right away, he just stood with an arm still around Rosie with a huge happy grin on his face.

It was Rosie who offered condolences.

"I had a really great partner." he said, smiling at Rosie.

"You two rode a really good race," Rosie said.

"Thanks," Sheryl responded. Then, a few minutes later, "Hey, Rosie, maybe we should think about putting together a women's Team Pursuit team for next Nationals. That Seattle gal and Kissena looked good, too! Maybe we could put together a winning team!"

"I'm in!" replied Rosie, happily with a smile. She'd love making that top podium spot, #1!

Just then, Rosie felt herself lifted off her feet.

"Great race, little girl!" crowed her dad. "Just like your old man!" he said proudly. "A winner!"

"I got it all from you, dad," she replied, laughing and hugging him back. She loved him to think that, even though she recognized that her calm persistence in athletics was as much due to her mother than her father. Mom was not as impulsive as dad. But Rosie felt the circle was completed, and she could see he was so proud. That made her as happy as winning the race.

"Hey Chill," Moocher hugged Chilly, "Great race! Are you okay?"

"Yeah, I'm good, dad." he said showing him his road rash.

Moocher looked intently, pulling at the skin around his injuries.

"Yeah, looks like you'll be okay. Great race, Chill."

The awards were the last event at this year's Grand Prix. All four of the Little 500 brothers stood by as their children along with wives and

mothers, real and by extension, receiving their medals and, as tradition dictated, their flowers. Everyone was proud. The Madison winnings were destined for college funds and bicycles. The fourth and fifth prizes were awarded because the race was such a good one.

Now it was time to EAT! Italian Style!

"See you there!" they all called to each other as they gathered up gear and strode off to the various vehicles for showers and clean up. What a great day!

The Letter

Dave pulled the letter out of his pocket again. He received it a week ago, but kept it in his pocket hoping that it would magically produce some sort of solution of how he could deal with it. He should have seen it coming, but he hadn't. Up until now, he almost felt he lead a charmed life. Racing was not easy, but he loved it so much, he almost loved the pain. When he began working for CinZano, his job didn't feel very important, but then he got a succession of opportunities that he grabbed with zeal and turned into even better opportunities. He had moved up the corporate ladder quickly and ended up as a sort of ombudsman, due to his talent with languages. When Gruppo Compari bought CinZano, another opportunity arrived, and he was up to the challenge.

The money poured in until he invested in the vineyard just to have a tax write-off -- and because he loved grapes. He had three varietals on his acreage, Chardonnay, Pinot Noir, and Merlot. All three were doing well until a movie called "Sideways" came out, with a mistaken message that Merlot made bad wine. The hero of "Sideways" actually hated Merlot because it was his ex-wife's favorite -- the woman with the exquisite palate -- but, viewers got the impression it was a bad wine and the bottom suddenly dropped out of the Merlot market. That caused a struggle.

Then his partner went bankrupt, went into "cahoots" with a con man, trying to steal the vineyard from him, and their winery declared bankruptcy after stiffing them for the second year. Dave didn't want to follow them to bankruptcy court. Meanwhile, there were bills to be paid. His temporary partner had done all he could, he didn't blame him. The notice in his pocket gave him one month to come up with a fair offer or the vineyard would be auctioned off. All of Dave's money was tied up, and there was no way he could raise that much within a month. He cursed himself for not seeing it sooner. As happy as he was to be at the track and with his brothers, this cloud over his head was with him every place he went. How could he tell Joelle? How could he pay for college for Joslyn? He was so used to having money, he was almost crippled, thinking about having to negotiate himself out of it. But he'd cry about that later. For now, he was happy to enjoy his "family", close and extended.

Awards and Rewards

The "boys" received an invitation mysteriously given to their wives by someone none of them knew, as they sat near the announcer's stand. Each was just a plain, simple, and unpretentious envelope, inviting the four of them to a coffeehouse the next morning. When the women asked, the messenger would only say "It's a surprise, I don't know either, I'm just the messenger." Nancy must have already gotten hers, she wasn't with the others by this time, she had left the track. Joelle took the invitations to the other side where the other "boys" sat with Dave's dad.

The next morning, in a meeting room of a hotel near the track, two people waited, looking at the invitations together. They had all enjoyed a great reunion dinner the night before, but when the evening ended, there was a feeling among the boys that there was something more to come, they weren't sure why.

"Yes, that's nice, exactly what I wanted it to look like. I hope they all come." they agreed, looking at the invitations.

"I hope so too", came the answer. "I know how important this is to you. You've been waiting for this day for a long time."

They smiled at each other and settled down to wait.

A hour later, the guys arrived at the time, one by one, at the place specified on the invitation. It was very mysterious, but Moocher had mentioned coffee the next morning and they guessed this was what he meant. It sounded like a mysterious adventure. Their wives were going to breakfast to spend more time together. They had enjoyed watching the racing together and all seemed comfortable with each other. Nancy had said she had business the next morning, so she'd be a little late.

Moocher was already at the coffeehouse as the others arrived. He greeted them, passing around some gourmet petite fours he'd made himself and some coffee and tea, awaiting their choice. What a great way to start a meeting!

Then, much to the others' surprise. Moocher got up and went to the head of the table. What was he doing up there? They thought they were going to get a real estate presentation or something. One of those "listen to our presentation and get a free night at our resort" or something like that. They didn't know.

"Hi guys," Moocher began, as he shuffled some envelopes in his hands. "I know you're all curious as to why I asked you to come here — yes, it was me. And Nancy, of course. The truth is, you are the main reason I came to Seattle, I figured you'd all be here, at least I hoped so." They looked at each other, surprised. Moocher? Since when did he send invitations? Oh, Nancy. That made sense.

Nancy came in and sat in a chair Moocher had placed in the corner. She was beaming. Was she pregnant again? No, that couldn't be. What WAS the deal?

Moocher didn't usually "take charge". He usually just let the others talk. Always congenial, he never sought center stage, but today was different, somehow. The others joked and nudged each other a little as they waited for him to reveal the reason for the invite, chuckling, nervous, afraid that Moocher was going to tell them he had cancer or something. He didn't seem like he was nervous or edgy, he seemed happy, happier than they'd ever seen him.

"You guys know I'm not usually the talker in the group. I'm usually the one listening to all of you. I learned a lot by listening. You know, I was worse off than any of you back in the old days. My mom died, my dad left town, and I had nothing except that awful old house, and even that was for sale, except that no one would buy it, it was in such bad shape. Things have changed for me 180 degrees since those days. No day has gone by that I wasn't grateful to you three for your friendship and your putting up with my temper and my constant lack of having anything to give. You were all so generous with me. I've waited all these years to pay you back."

The others started talking over each other, in harmony, and in protest. "You don't need to do anything for us, we're fine, we're all fine! We're just glad things worked out with you and Nancy! You have a great family, we don't need anything, really. It's great to see you, Mooch."

The waiter came in, carrying more refreshments. The men passed the tray around, getting ready for... whatever it was. Moocher stood his ground, literally. He looked at them and waited until they ran out of things to say.

"Don't ruin my big moment! Please, let me do what I want to do today. Please give me the pleasure of allowing me to do something for you, this time. It would make me the happiest man in the world, if you'd just accept what I have to give. You know that our relationship was never about money, ever. Heck, in those days none of us had any! But you helped me survive with the small amount you each had, and I've always been so grateful, so wanting to pay you back in some way, not with money, but with love. There is such a thing as giving to someone else by accepting what they have to give. I'm asking you -- BEGGING you -- to give to me by accepting what I want to give to you. There is no debt here, just an expression of love for my best brothers."

The "boys" looked around, finding it very hard to understand this sharp change in their perceptions of their place in this four-way relationship. Taking from Moocher? It always made them feel good to have HIM accept from THEM! They liked it that way and this new idea of accepting from a guy they never knew to have two pennies to rub together was a whole new idea. They looked at each other. Mike spoke first.

"Okay, Moocher, I understand. So does this mean we can't call you "Moocher" any more?"

Moocher laughed. "No, no, I'll always be happy to go by "Moocher". I don't know how I'd get used to any other name anyway. I always hated "Wolfgang"."

The boys broke up with laughter, including Moocher. "Wolfgang? Your parents named you Wolfgang?"

"Hey, my mom was German. She had a favorite uncle in the old country named Wolfgang and she named me after him. He used to come visit, and he was a great guy, but it wasn't a name I ever wanted. It's a great German name, but it never went over very well in the US. Moocher sounded like a great name to me. I didn't know what it meant at first, but

I didn't mind, as long as they didn't call me Wolfgang. A teacher sort of gave it to me in Kindergarten because I used to beg the other kids for food at lunch time. I was always hungry. I thought it would help me grow, but that didn't work out."

The boys settled down, still chuckling.

"Anyway, let's get to business." and the group quieted down.

"Let me do this in order." said Moocher, laying out three envelopes in front of him."

"Could I say something?" Nancy asked, from her corner.

"Sure" said Moocher. The boys turned.

"Just real quick. I'm not supposed to be part of this except I asked Moocher if I could sit in. I want you all to know how long Moocher's planned this and with what joy in his heart he loved dreaming about this day all these years. We'd both really appreciate it if you would just let him do this and just feel the love that you gave him all those years ago."

The guys agreed, looking at each other, that they would accept whatever was coming, with no complaints. Surely it couldn't be much, and if Moocher wanted to give it, okay, let him.

"Okay, Mooch, okay, do what you want and we'll cooperate" Mike said, looking at the others, who were nodding their agreement. Mike said it with an air of authority that any reservations by the others disappeared.

"Okay, now remember, you promised.' he looked around, waiting for any retractions. "Here goes."

"First, Cyril." He cleared his throat.

"Cyril, you were always with me in the back seat of Mike's car. Even though you were so big, and hardly fit yourself, you always gave me room, handed me towels and jackets, shared your food with me and so many small, generous things that you didn't know I noticed. I noticed. Some days were really tough, but you always slipped me a few bucks or some food that you needed for yourself. I was so desperate, I chalked up each of your kind acts into dreams of something I thought that I could do for you some day. It wasn't easy. I know you're successful and all, so I don't want you to be offended, but when I saw this, I decided it was just what I had in mind -- even though I had no idea what I had in mind -- this is just what would make me happy to give you. I knew it the minute I saw it. You know, when Nancy showed it to me as one suggestion."

" Now I want you to understand, really, this isn't costing me ANY money, it's not about money. This is just something I want you to get from me, well, actually from Nancy, but from us both. Here, go ahead and open your envelope." and he handed Cyril the envelope marked "Cyril".

Cyril opened his envelope and took out what looked like a set of travel vouchers. He opened it further and found a "Carte Blanche" ticket for any five star resort in the world, one week, all expenses paid, yearly, for the next 10 years — or sooner, if he chose. He was stunned.

"How did you... ?? This must have cost a fortune!" Moocher couldn't afford things like this. Why did he give this to him? How did he get the money? Why wasn't he using it for himself?

"Look, Mooch," Cyril said solemnly. "I appreciate the offer, but I can't take this. We have enough money to do these kinds of things. Sure, we have to plan ahead, it's not like we're rich, college profs don't make a ton of money, but our grants pay for our research in foreign places, we get to travel. I really appreciate this, but really, I don't know how you can afford it. You and Nancy must be able to use it. You need to use it."

"I know you mean that sincerely, Cyril, but let me tell you why you need to use it. Nancy won it as Manager of the Year, 10 years running. One week, the foreign place of your choice all expenses paid. You can do research while you're there if you want! But we don't want it, really, and I couldn't think of anyone I'd rather give it to than you -- it's already paid for — it's one of those business incentive deals, with no time limit. It pays for the flight and the resort, food included. The commitment just sits there, ready to be used, all at once or in parts. We're obviously not going to use it. Nancy doesn't work for awards, she just happens to love her work and be very good at it. Knowing her, she'll win more. Dave and Mike have both traveled a lot, they've seen the world, but you and Melody have had your nose in the books so much, I know you haven't traveled as much as you'd like. You were saying how you'd like to travel without having to plan time to attend some convention and present your latest paper. Here's your chance. You and Melody go on that honeymoon you never got and enjoy yourselves. You can pick a better place to vacation than we would and you'd enjoy it more. We love our life in Bloomington and we have the kids, the shop, Nancy's job, we don't want or need this kind of thing and we would be SO happy if you'd take it. There are TWO conditions: You need to bring back souvenirs for each of the kids, and send pictures of the places you visit."

Cyril looked down at the ticket in his hands. Hmmm, being able to "give back" helped Moocher's persuasion. He understood how giving could feel good. Maybe he could include some research while he was...

No, DON'T think of that, this is a gift, and he'd promised to accept it. Hawaii? Europe? India?

"It would be great to just GO, without worrying about what time we need to get up and give our presentations at whatever conference we elected to go to at whatever city the college chose. We could do some of the traveling we wanted." There were always so many classes to teach and papers to correct, they could never just relax and enjoy each other's company. Melody would LOVE it, she was always talking about places she'd like to go -- so Cyril would too.

"I don't know what to say, Mooch. It would be a great trip, no doubt. I understand about your life in Bloomington, though. When you're happy in a certain place -- like Colorado -- you don't really need to leave. Now that Marie is growing up and she'll be off to college, she doesn't need us around all the time any more anyway. I'll tell you what, we'll also bring things back for you and Nancy, just like you went with us. We'll keep in touch by email and the net and take LOTS of pictures. If you will make me happy by accepting that deal, I'll be happy to show Melody what a great pal I have in you. You can travel with me without leaving Bloomington. It's a deal. Thanks so much, Mooch, this is really great. Gee, a whole week of fun with no obligations. Maybe we'll take a trip around the world! We could!"

"I'll REALLY love looking at those pictures, Cyril. Just figure you're taking them for us on the trip we would LOVE to take -- as long as we don't have to leave Bloomington!"

"Thanks, Moocher, that's really great. I promise you, we'll tell you all about it."

Mike and Dave squirmed a little. They didn't need trips, they'd already traveled so much, all they wanted is a place to STAY.

"Mike you're next", said Moocher.

Moocher handed Mike his envelope. Mike opened it. It appeared to be a check. For a LOT of money, tens of thousands of dollars. Mike did NOT want Moocher's money.

"What? Are you crazy? I don't want your money! Here, take this

back, I don't need your money, what, are you trying to insult me? Here!"
and he threw the check at Moocher with contempt. "I can provide for my
family I make lots of money in the military!" which Moocher knew was
a lie, but he let it slide.

"Mike, you don't understand. Listen a minute. Listen to me.
Look in the envelope" He waited a minute, anticipating Mike's reaction.
Mike hadn't gotten all the paperwork out of the envelope. "Remember
when you were helping us fix up our first house? Remember?"

"Yeah, I remember, I remember doing it because you were my
FRIEND, not because of any damn money you didn't have. I don't want
this!" He protested. And, in a low whisper, "...besides, I didn't really
have anything else to do and it gave me something to do. Don't insult
me."

"Look, Mike. Let me explain a few more things. You worked on
our house with me for almost a year, until you joined the Corps. I really
appreciated it, and I KNOW you didn't do it with money in mind. But
the way I figured it, you bought into ownership of the house, you know,
just like you owned part of it for all the work you did for no pay,
especially building the new garage. That's what I was thinking at the
time. Your work bought you a percentage, and Nancy and I used to talk
about it after you went home. We figured you bought in about 25%. Well,
we finally sold the old place and this is simply a return on your
investment. Look at that paper of the sale. Don't worry, we got plenty
too! This is just 25%, we're keeping 50%, the other 25% went to my dad.
It's fair!"

Nancy interrupted at this point: "Mike, we talked about it way
back then. We both felt bad we couldn't pay you in any way, but you did
SO much work! We wanted to at least pay you in food, but most of the
time, you wouldn't even take that. So we agreed that when we sold the
old house, you would get one-fourth of the proceeds. It's as simple as
that. You EARNED it. We just didn't tell you until now. It was strictly a
business deal. Yes, I know it feels like we're giving you money, but
really, we're just paying you your share."

Mike didn't know how to argue that. He could see that they
really wanted to give it to him. When they put it like that, maybe he did
deserve it. He could use it, these days, if he admitted it, that's for sure,
but he didn't want them to know how much that was true.

"Give to me by accepting what I give, Mike." Moocher insisted.

"We all know you deserve it, and it would make us very happy if you'd take it. Buy Rosie a new bike or something! Bikes these days could eat up that money fast!"

"Wait a minute. Let me think about this..." Mike got quiet and shut the others out while he considered.

Ahhhh there was the clincher (pun intended - clincher is a type of bike tire). Buy things for Rosie. Things that would otherwise be hard for him to afford. There was plenty in the check for a new bike, for Rosie, himself, and several others! He would love to buy Rosie the bikes she wanted, especially now that she showed how good she was getting at racing. She told him she needed a couple of different bikes for different events. They were specialized racing bicycles and REALLY expensive. He already felt bad he couldn't afford to buy them for her. He'd been thinking of how he could borrow money for her for all the trips and equipment she needed. Now he could, and without borrowing! He wanted to make up for all that time he'd been away from her. He sat there a few minutes, quiet. Thinking. The others honored his need to think and consider as they waited, chatting quietly about places Cyril could go. Mike could see that Moocher and Nancy really meant it, and if they just paid him out of proceeds from that old house, well, that might be okay. Wow, they'd gotten a good chunk of change, too. The others held their breath, knowing how much Moocher wanted him to accept and knowing how volatile he was about everything.

Mike thought back on the time he spent working on Moocher's dad's house. What Moocher didn't know is that working on that old house was the ONLY thing that kept him sane and made him feel like his existence was worth anything, by getting up and going to do that work every day, even with no pay -- or maybe especially with no pay. In those darkest of days, Moocher and that old house were the only light. But, he could see how sincere Moocher was, so he'd accept it.

"Okay, Mooch, I'll take it, but when you watch Rosie win races, know that it's YOUR bike that she's winning on! I'll take it for HER."

"Great, Mike. Thank you for accepting it. I'll look for Rosie and her gear! You know, with the shop, I can get stuff for you wholesale!" Moocher said with relief. He thought Mike would be the tough one to accept his "award". He would be finding out that Mike was easy compared to his last friend, Dave. Mike chuckled and put the check in his wallet.

"**Dave, it's your turn** to open your envelope."

Dave was dying with curiosity, but the last thing he needed was a trip around the world. Was it money? He could sure use that, but Moocher would never be able to come up with the amount that no one knew he desperately needed. Well, that's okay, whatever Moocher wanted to give, he was fine with accepting it. It couldn't be too much, Moocher and Nancy were always broke. He hadn't seen what Mike got, and really didn't want to know. That was Mike's business.

He opened the envelope. He was stunned and stupefied into staring for a full minute and a half -- which is a long time when people are waiting for your reaction. The others could hardly contain themselves, but they forced themselves to wait.

"Moocher, are you KIDDING???" Dave exploded.

Moocher started to laugh. Nancy suddenly burst into laughter too. They kept laughing, almost hysterically. After a minute or two, they quieted down. Mike and Cyril tried hard to subtly look over Dave's shoulder to see what Moocher gave him, but they couldn't see it. They could see it was a check and some sort of legal papers, but they couldn't see anything more. They tried to be patient.

"What? What is it?" they demanded, almost in unison.

"I don't get it" said Dave. "Where did this come from? You can't afford this. I don't understand."

Moocher and Nancy started to laugh again.

"Do you want to tell him, Nancy, or should I?" asked Moocher.

"You'd better tell him," Nancy replied "he may not believe me."

"Here's what none of you know." Moocher began. "Nancy and I have always been very frugal with our money, you know that. Neither of us have ever needed to show off or buy big fancy cars. We get around Bloomington by bicycle a lot of the time. The bike paths are great. We don't take long trips. We bought the old house from my dad. Part of the deal was his retaining one-fourth of the ownership. We just finally sold that place. But all the years since, we bought another house... then another one... and gradually, over the years, we became owners of quite a few houses in Bloomington. Over half are located near the university, so we rent them out to students all the time. They have largely paid for themselves."

Nancy chimed in: "Yes and while I made money working, so did Moocher. He fixed up the houses, one by one, while taking care of the

146

kids. The fact is, I know we don't look like it, but we're actually rich. We don't want people to know, because money makes people act funny. We just want to be plain folks, and if we end up with a lot of money, that's fine, but the money can just sit there. We're happy just being like we are.

We just got into a habit of frugality from the beginning, since we didn't have anything, and we've really enjoyed saving every nickel and dime. We put our money in real estate and a few stocks and bonds. Just a little at a time, but we don't spend, and it's built up. I think they call it "buried money", money that people have, but it's sort of "below ground", in banks, investments and real estate, so it's not noticeable that you have it. We can tell you because we know you don't care one way or the other. We've been very fortunate in our choices. We can afford to move our money around a little. So Dave, we heard you were in trouble and with a vineyard, which really sounds like fun! It wasn't hard for us to get, all the banks know us, plus, we have more than that stashed away. We DO want something in return, though. Strictly business." Nancy said.

"Uh oh, here it comes", thought Dave, his happy bubble, at this possibility of saving him, deflating a little.

"We know you don't want a handout, Dave, we get that. But Moocher was talking to your dad, and he explained the situation. We want to buy into your vineyard, buy out the partner that you have right now, assuming we can negotiate a buy-out. If you want, you can put our names on the title or just do a note and pay us back at your leisure." Nancy concluded. "We don't need the money and it will be a great tax write off. We do need those!"

"Which would you prefer?" asked Dave. "Silent partner or "real" partner?

"Actually, we'd enjoy being silent partners in your vineyard. Run it the way you want, we take a tax write-off, and come help with harvest every Fall, bringing all the kids! To tell you the truth, we thought it would be a great thing for the kids to do in the summer, work on the vineyard and help with harvest. It sounds like the house is big enough, we could come like summer camp!" Moocher said.

"Wine!" exalted Cyril. "Melody and I love wine tasting!"

Dave and Mike just looked at each other.

"Nope, sorry, Cyril, no wine. This is strictly a vineyard." Dave said. "We do sell to wineries, truc, but it's really all about the grapes. Fresh grapes off the vine are heaven and farming is so interesting. Best time of the year is harvest time."

"Oh," commented Cyril. "Well, that's okay, all that fresh oxygen and sunshine, it has to be healthy."

"Definitely," answered Dave. "And peaceful!"

Dave would have to think about this. As much as it was breaking his heart, he had almost regretfully accepted that he would have to let the vineyard go. The thought of his best friends being part of it was like reentering heaven. Partners? Money? How did they do that? They probably have more money than I do, but I need to think about this, he thought quietly.

"Give me 24 hours?" Dave asked. "I need to talk to my dad about this."

"Sure, we understand", chimed Moocher and Nancy. "Take all the time you need. We're here for you, Dave. Do what you need to do."

Handsling Philosophy

Dave had a hard time trying to find a negative aspect to saving his precious vineyard. Deep inside, he looked forward to the idea of Moocher and Nancy and the kids all coming for the summers. Cyril and Mike and their families could come too! Any time!

They went to join their families at breakfast. Dave wanted to find his dad and run the whole thing by him and his mom, too.

"Can I come with you when you talk to your dad?" asked Mike. "I'd like to hear what the old guy has to say."

"Sure, Mike. As you know, he's full of surprises." said Dave.

Dave and Mike found Dave's dad on the other side of the track. They hadn't needed to be in the middle of things, they just enjoyed the show and the great Seattle cuisine. They were having some special kids training events, and Dave's parents loved watching them.

Dave handed his dad a special brew of decaf tea that they were selling at the velodrome. Dave wanted to support the new company.

"The guy I bought this tea from said that if you didn't like it, he'd give you a refund." Dave advised.

"Refund? Refund!? I sure will ask him for one if I don't like this tea. Organic is it? Sometimes that's good, sometimes it's not. I like refunds, as long as I'm not the one who has to give them!" he said emphatically, while Dave and Mike laughed. They knew how much he meant that.

"So hey, sit down," Mr Stohler said, congenially. "Take a load off and tell me what's going on." He patted the seats next to him.

Dave's mother just smiled her lovely smile.

Dave explained about Moocher's offer and the surprise that a guy like Moocher turned out to have enough money to undertake a whole new enterprise like a vineyard. Moocher had grown family food since he and Nancy got married, so he knew a lot about growing things, though not so much about grapes. But he was a quick study and loved farming. Dave recounted his reservations and mixed emotions.

His dad sat for a few minutes, then sat up to give his best advice.

"Let me tell you what I've been reflecting on while I've been here and watching all these races, son, especially when I was watching that Madison race. I've been reading a little about this Jerry Baker fella, the man this track is named after. One of the parents told me more about him, how important he'd been to the people here. I've realized a lot of things over the last day or two. "

"Here's the thing" he continued, "We're all connected. Everyone gives something to those around them, even when they have NO idea they're doing it. I watched the way one rider grabs the other and flings him into the race. I understand that's called a "handsling". Life's is full of handslings. We're all grabbed by something and flung into the future, ready or not. All you can do is pump like mad, hope you don't get knocked down, and try to do the best you can to stay up!"

"You know that "Little 500" you boys raced all those years ago? That race threw each of you into futures that you didn't plan. Hell, it even threw me into something I didn't have planned."

Dave knew he meant Angelina and his larger car dealership.

"Dave won a bike race and wound up working for a team that lead to an international career and a vineyard. Moocher got married and had a son who wanted to race like his dad, so Moocher ended up with a bike shop and a whole lot more. Cyril met a girl who loved bicycling, and who figured he knew a lot about that -- well, you know, Cyril didn't know anything about it, and he still doesn't, but it still got her interested, and that's all that needed to happen. You guys didn't plan to win that race -- well, Dave did, but the rest of you didn't, but look what happened. It didn't seem like much, at the time, but there it was, a little ingredient that influenced your whole life.

"Mike, your first handsling after the 500 was when the group split up. You poured your energy into helping Moocher with his house, not going out and getting drunk or anything stupid like that. You stayed in shape. Your next handsling was meeting Henry and joining the Corps. When Rosie took up bike racing, she ended up a lot like you, competitive and with something to prove. So here you are, getting to watch her be the girl you partly determined her to be. Ferocious. Determined. Strong. A person who fights, and fights hard."

"You got hurt in Iraq. You didn't ask for it, you did your duty. Today, if you ask me, you're getting hand-slung into getting help you've needed for some time if you just grab Cyril's hand, so to speak. He's reaching out and he's trained to help. You'd never have expected that. I know Marines, they're proud, too proud to admit when they need help. You're a good man and deserve to be as happy as anyone, so I hope you'll reach forward and grab Cyril's hand to let him throw you back into the race. If you don't, you know these guys, one of them will grab your "jamming tool" and fling you in anyway!" They laughed.

"Dave, your next handsling is Moocher -- Moocher, of all people! -- helping you save your vineyard. You know he loves to help you, and you all can get together every year or more, at a nice place and pick grapes, eat and learn to farm. It can be like Little Italy."

"We all get into places where life comes down, grabs us and flings us into our futures. If you're lucky, you have some friends who are still with you in the race."

"We don't know what that future will bring, but sometimes we don't have any choice. What takes us anywhere is only partly what we decide. The rest is a handsling. You're in that place now again, all of you. I know none of us expected Moocher to be the guy slinging you all in, but that's the beauty of the race, you just never know how it's going to turn out."

They all sat in silence for a few minutes. Dave saw no better alternative for any of them than to share the vineyard. With partners, they could do it.

"You're right, dad. And I never found any better family than the guys from Bloomington." said Dave. Mike shook his head in agreement.

"Maybe I'll just grab Moocher's hand and let him throw me in." said Dave with a smile.

Mr Stohler nodded. "It might work — or, you'll have a really good time finding out. "

The Handsling of the Jerry Baker Kiddie Kilo

They sat for a while, watching a group of children that included Angelina's kids getting ready for the Jerry Baker "Kiddie Kilo". They were so excited! Each child would ride a short race on the velodrome to the cheers of a wide audience. Some children only had a push bike and were three years old. Others were 8 or 9. All looked happy and ready to emulate the racing they had seen (minus handslings).

"Imagine how many of those little kids are getting their handsling into racing in the future right now because of Jerry Baker, who devoted his whole life to something he loved? Now he has a race and a velodrome named after him and some of those kids we're watching may end up National or even World Champions. That man's influence is still slinging people in to racing bicycles and just having fun riding even though he's not here any more. Parents come just so their kids will have fun at this event, learning about bicycling in other ways or just having fun with their friends. This is so good for kids. You never know how long what you do might last, sometimes it lasts for way longer than you do!" said Mr Stohler with a smile.

"Adorable!" exclaimed Mrs Stohler as she watched her grandchildren and the others get ready with their bikes. By this time, the all the guys, wives, and children were back together.

As Dave and Mike watched the happy children and their equally happy parents, they knew Dave's dad was right. Life slings you in. All you can do is pedal like hell and try to stay up.

As he signed the papers, unifying all the boys again, Dave knew he had finally found his Italian family that stayed together -- in truth, he had always had it.

Jerry Baker - Seattle Icon

Jerry Baker was the "rock" of the Marymoor Velodrome, the man who was always there, through thick and thin. He was part of making the velodrome a reality when it was built in 1976, always with suggestions and ideas of how to make the bicycling experience better. There were attempts to name the Marymoor Velodrome after him before he left us, but the city said "No, not while the person's still living." Jerry knew that many planned that he would be honored in this way.

I met Jerry at the time of the 1986 Nationals, when my friend Jean Laffen and I volunteered. I had heard about Jerry all the way down in San Diego before even coming to Seattle. Jerry/Baleno purchased some copies of the first bicycle book I ever did, *Bicycle Training for the Triathlete *and Others* (1983) (with Audrey McElmury and Michael Levonas). When the 1991 Goodwill Games were held, he helped me gain permission to take photos from restricted vantage points. I did my first photo exhibit from photos taken at Marymoor with Jerry's support. He loaned me a display stand he used when selling Baleno merchandise. It was put together ingeniously, and he showed me how. From there I did photo exhibits at Nationals yearly for 10 years. When I was preparing my book, *NO BRAKES! Bicycle Track Racing in the United States*, (1996), Jerry advised me on a few crucial items. The last time I saw him, in 2015, he proudly told me of his 36th ride of the Seattle to Portland bike ride. He never missed it.

I don't doubt that Jerry would be supportive about the effort in this book to re-enter this fictional world of the Cutters that intrigued us all from 1979 to today. Of course it was set at the Jerry Baker Marymoor Velodrome. I renamed it the Jerry Baker Velodrome prior to Jerry's unexpected death. I looked forward to showing it to him and his almost shy chuckle at my doing this. I know he's up... wherever he is... chuckling at the fun. Last time we spoke, he noted: "Bicycling keeps us young." So true.

Jerry's special event was the Kiddie Kilo, which everyone loves. He knew where the strength of bicycling's future comes from: the children. I know Jerry's legacy will continue indefinitely, handslinging many children into involvement with bicycling through his life's work, which is the main message of *Handsling*. Those who contribute to our lives in unique and special ways help create our futures. If we stay upright and keep pedaling hard, there's no telling what might happen.

Thank you, Jerry. You'll never be forgotten.

Sandra Wright Sutherland

Index